The Commission in Lunacy

Honore de Balzac

Contents

THE COMMISSION
IN LUNACY

BY

Honore de Balzac

THE COMMISSION IN LUNACY

In 1828, at about one o'clock one morning, two persons came out of a large house in the Rue du Faubourg Saint-Honore, near the Elysee-Bourbon. One was the famous doctor, Horace Bianchon; the other was one of the most elegant men in Paris, the Baron de Rastignac; they were friends of long standing. Each had sent away his carriage, and no cab was to be seen in the street; but the night was fine, and the pavement dry.

"We will walk as far as the boulevard," said Eugene de Rastignac to Bianchon. "You can get a hackney cab at the club; there is always one to be found there till daybreak. Come with me as far as my house."

"With pleasure."

"Well, and what have you to say about it?"

"About that woman?" said the doctor coldly.

"There I recognize my Bianchon!" exclaimed Rastignac.

"Why, how?"

"Well, my dear fellow, you speak of the Marquise d'Espard as if she were a case for your hospital."

"Do you want to know what I think, Eugene? If you throw over Madame de Nucingen for this Marquise, you will swap a one-eyed horse for a blind one."

"Madame de Nucingen is six-and-thirty, Bianchon."

"And this woman is three-and-thirty," said the doctor quickly.

"Her worst enemies only say six-and-twenty."

"My dear boy, when you really want to know a woman's age, look at her temples and the tip of her nose. Whatever women may achieve with their cosmetics, they can do nothing against those incorruptible witnesses to their experiences. There each year of life has left its stigmata. When a woman's temples are flaccid, seamed, withered in a particular way; when at the tip of her nose you see those minute specks, which look like the imperceptible black smuts which are shed in London by the chimneys in which coal is burnt. . . . Your servant, sir! That woman is more than thirty. She may be handsome, witty, loving --whatever you please, but she is past thirty, she is arriving at maturity. I do not blame men who attach themselves to that kind of woman; only, a man of your superior distinction must not mistake a winter pippin for a little summer apple, smiling on the bough, and waiting for you to crunch it. Love never goes to study the registers of birth and marriage; no one loves a woman because she is handsome or ugly, stupid or clever; we love because we love."

"Well, for my part, I love for quite other reasons. She is Marquise d'Espard; she was a Blamont-Chauvry; she is the fashion; she has soul; her foot is as pretty as the Duchesse de Berri's; she has perhaps a hundred thousand francs a year--some day, perhaps, I may marry her! In short, she will put me into a position which will enable me to pay my debts."

"I thought you were rich," interrupted Bianchon.

"Bah! I have twenty thousand francs a year--just enough to keep up my stables. I was thoroughly done, my dear fellow, in that Nucingen business; I will tell you about that.--I have got my sisters married; that is the clearest profit I can show since we last met; and I would rather have them provided for than have five hundred thousand francs a year. No, what would you have me do? I am ambitious. To what can Madame de Nucingen lead? A year more and I shall be shelved, stuck in a pigeon-hole like a married man. I have all the discomforts of marriage and of single life, without the advantages of either; a false position to which every man must come who remains tied too long to the same apron-string."

"So you think you will come upon a treasure here?" said Bianchon. "Your Marquise, my dear fellow, does not hit my fancy at all."

"Your liberal opinions blur your eyesight. If Madame d'Espard were a Madame Rabourdin . . ."

"Listen to me. Noble or simple, she would still have no soul; she would still be a perfect type of selfishness. Take my word for it, medical men are accustomed to judge of people and things; the sharpest of us read the soul while we study the body. In spite of that pretty boudoir where we have spent this evening, in spite of the magnificence of the house, it is quite possible that Madame la Marquise is in debt."

"What makes you think so?"

"I do not assert it; I am supposing. She talked of her soul as Louis XVIII. used to talk of his heart. I tell you this: That fragile, fair woman, with her chestnut hair, who pities herself that she may be pitied, enjoys an iron constitution, an appetite like a wolf's, and the strength and cowardice of a tiger. Gauze, and silk, and muslin were never more cleverly twisted round a lie! Ecco."

"Bianchon, you frighten me! You have learned a good many things, then, since we lived in the Maison Vauquer?"

"Yes, since then, my boy, I have seen puppets, both dolls and manikins. I know something of the ways of the fine ladies whose bodies we attend to, saving that which is dearest to them, their child--if they love it--or their pretty faces, which they always worship. A man spends his nights by their pillow, wearing himself to death to spare them the slightest loss of beauty in any part; he succeeds, he keeps their secret like the dead; they send to ask for his bill, and think it horribly exorbitant. Who saved them? Nature. Far from recommending him, they speak ill of him, fearing lest he should become the physician of their best friends.

"My dear fellow, those women of whom you say, 'They are angels!' I --I--have seen stripped of the little grimaces under which they hide their soul, as well as of the frippery under which they disguise their defects--without manners and without stays; they are not beautiful.

"We saw a great deal of mud, a great deal of dirt, under the waters of the world when we were aground for a time on the shoals of the Maison Vauquer.--What we saw there was nothing. Since I have gone into high society, I have seen monsters dressed in satin, Michonneaus in white gloves, Poirets bedizened with orders, fine gentlemen doing more usurious business than old Gobseck! To the shame of mankind, when I have wanted to shake hands with Virtue, I have found her shivering in a loft, persecuted by calumny, half-starving on a income or a salary of fifteen hundred francs a year, and regarded as crazy, or eccentric, or imbecile.

"In short, my dear boy, the Marquise is a woman of fashion, and I have a particular horror of that kind of woman. Do you want to know why? A woman who has a lofty soul, fine taste, gentle wit, a generously warm heart, and who lives a simple life, has not a chance of being the fashion. Ergo: A woman of fashion and a man in power are analogous; but there is this difference: the qualities by which a man raises himself above others ennoble him and are a glory to him; whereas the qualities by which a woman gains power for a day are hideous vices; she belies her nature to hide her character, and to live the militant life of the world she must have iron strength under a frail appearance.

"I, as a physician, know that a sound stomach excludes a good heart. Your woman of fashion feels nothing; her rage for pleasure has its source in a longing to heat up her cold nature, a craving for excitement and enjoyment, like an old man who stands night after night by the footlights at the opera. As she has more brain than heart, she sacrifices genuine passion and true friends to her triumph, as a general sends his most devoted subalterns to the front in order to win a battle. The woman of fashion ceases to be a woman; she is neither mother, nor wife, nor lover. She is, medically speaking, sex in the brain. And your Marquise, too, has all the characteristics of her monstrosity, the beak of a bird of prey, the clear, cold eye, the gentle voice--she is as polished as the steel of a machine, she touches everything except the heart."

"There is some truth in what you say, Bianchon."

"Some truth?" replied Bianchon. "It is all true. Do you suppose that I was not struck to the heart by the insulting politeness by which she made me measure the imaginary distance which her noble birth sets between us? That I did not feel the deepest pity for her cat-like civilities when I remembered what her object was? A year hence she will not write one word to do me the slightest service, and this evening she pelted me with smiles, believing that I can influence my uncle Popinot, on whom the success of her case----"

"Would you rather she should have played the fool with you, my dear fellow?--I accept your diatribe against women of fashion; but you are beside the mark. I should always prefer for a wife a Marquise d'Espard to the most devout and devoted creature on earth. Marry an angel! you would have to go and bury your happiness in the depths of the country! The wife of a politician is a governing machine, a contrivance that makes compliments and courtesies. She is the most important and most faithful tool which an ambitious man can use; a friend, in short, who may compromise herself without mischief, and whom he may belie without harmful results. Fancy Mahomet in Paris in the nineteenth century! His wife would be a Rohan, a Duchesse de Chevreuse of the Fronde, as keen and as flattering as an Ambassadress, as wily as Figaro. Your loving wives lead nowhere; a woman of the world leads to everything; she is the diamond with which a man cuts every window when he has not the golden key which unlocks every door. Leave humdrum virtues to the humdrum, ambitious vices to the ambitious.

"Besides, my dear fellow, do you imagine that the love of a Duchesse de Langeais, or de Maufrigneuse, or of a Lady Dudley does not bestow immense pleasure? If only you knew how much value the cold, severe style of such a woman gives to the smallest evidence of their affection! What a delight it is to see a periwinkle piercing through the snow! A smile from below a fan contradicts the reserve of an assumed attitude, and is worth all the unbridled tenderness of your middle-class women with their mortgaged devotion; for, in love, devotion is nearly akin to speculation.

"And, then, a woman of fashion, a Blamont-Chauvry, has her virtues too! Her virtues are fortune, power, effect, a certain contempt of all that is beneath her----"

"Thank you!" said Bianchon.

"Old curmudgeon!" said Rastignac, laughing. "Come--do not be so common, do like your friend Desplein; be a Baron, a Knight of Saint-Michael; become a peer of France, and marry your daughters to dukes."

"I! May the five hundred thousand devils----"

"Come, come! Can you be superior only in medicine? Really, you distress me . . ."

"I hate that sort of people; I long for a revolution to deliver us from them for ever."

"And so, my dear Robespierre of the lancet, you will not go to-morrow to your uncle Popinot?"

"Yes, I will," said Bianchon; "for you I would go to hell to fetch water . . ."

"My good friend, you really touch me. I have sworn that a commission shall sit on the Marquis. Why, here is even a long-saved tear to thank you."

"But," Bianchon went on, "I do not promise to succeed as you wish with Jean-Jules Popinot. You do not know him. However, I will take him to see your Marquise the day after to-morrow; she may get round him if she can. I doubt it. If all the truffles, all the Duchesses, all the mistresses, and all the charmers in Paris were there in the full bloom of their beauty; if the King promised him the /Prairie/, and the Almighty gave him the Order of Paradise with the revenues of Purgatory, not one of all these powers would induce him to transfer a single straw from one saucer of his scales into the other. He is a judge, as Death is Death."

The two friends had reached the office of the Minister for Foreign Affairs, at the corner of the Boulevard des Capucines.

"Here you are at home," said Bianchon, laughing, as he pointed to the ministerial residence. "And here is my carriage," he added, calling a hackney cab. "And these--express our fortune."

"You will be happy at the bottom of the sea, while I am still struggling with the tempests on the surface, till I sink and go to ask you for a corner in your grotto, old fellow!"

"Till Saturday," replied Bianchon.

"Agreed," said Rastignac. "And you promise me Popinot?"

"I will do all my conscience will allow. Perhaps this appeal for a commission covers some little dramorama, to use a word of our good bad times."

"Poor Bianchon! he will never be anything but a good fellow," said Rastignac to himself as the cab drove off.

"Rastignac has given me the most difficult negotiation in the world," said Bianchon to himself, remembering, as he rose next morning, the delicate commission intrusted to him. "However, I have never asked the smallest service from my uncle in Court, and have paid more than a thousand visits gratis for him. And, after all, we are not apt to mince matters between ourselves. He will say Yes or No, and there an end."

After this little soliloquy the famous physician bent his steps, at seven in the morning, towards the Rue du Fouarre, where dwelt Monsieur Jean-Jules Popinot, judge of the Lower Court of the Department of the Seine. The Rue du Fouarre--an old word meaning straw--was in the thirteenth century the most important street in Paris. There stood the Schools of the University, where the voices of Abelard and of Gerson were heard in the world of learning. It is now one of the dirtiest streets of the Twelfth Arrondissement, the poorest quarter of Paris, that in which two-thirds of the population lack firing in winter, which leaves most brats at the gate of the Foundling Hospital, which sends most beggars to the poorhouse, most rag-pickers to the street corners, most decrepit old folks to bask against the walls on which the sun shines, most delinquents to the police courts.

Half-way down this street, which is always damp, and where the gutter carries to the Seine the blackened waters from some dye-works, there is an old house, restored no doubt under Francis I., and built of bricks held together by a few courses of masonry. That it is substantial seems proved by the shape of its front wall, not uncommonly seen in some parts of Paris. It bellies, so to speak, in a manner caused by the protuberance of its first floor, crushed under the weight of the second and third, but upheld by the strong wall of the ground floor. At first sight it would seem as though the piers between the windows, though strengthened by the stone mullions, must give way, but the observer presently perceives that, as in the tower at Bologna, the old bricks and old time-eaten stones of this house persistently preserve their centre of gravity.

At every season of the year the solid piers of the ground floor have the yellow tone and the imperceptible sweating surface that moisture gives to stone. The passer-by feels chilled as he walks close to this wall, where worn corner-stones ineffectually shelter him from the wheels of vehicles. As is always the case in houses built before carriages were in use, the vault of the doorway forms a very low archway not unlike the barbican of a prison. To the right of this entrance there are three windows, protected outside by iron gratings of so close a pattern, that the curious cannot possibly see the use made of the dark, damp rooms within, and the panes too are dirty and dusty; to the left are two similar windows, one of which is sometimes open, exposing to view the porter, his wife, and his children; swarming, working, cooking, eating, and screaming, in a floored and wainscoted room where everything is dropping to pieces, and into which you descend two steps--a depth which seems to suggest the gradual elevation of the soil of Paris.

If on a rainy day some foot-passenger takes refuge under the long vault, with projecting lime-washed beams, which leads from the door to the staircase, he will hardly fail to pause and look at the picture presented by the interior of this house. To the left is a square garden-plot, allowing of not more than four long steps in each direction, a garden of black soil, with trellises bereft of vines, and where, in default of vegetation under the shade of two trees, papers collect, old rags, potsherds, bits of mortar fallen from the roof; a barren ground, where time has shed on the walls, and on the trunks and branches of the trees, a powdery deposit like cold soot. The two parts of the house, set at a right angle, derive light from this garden-court shut in by two adjoining houses built on wooden piers, decrepit and ready to fall, where on each floor some grotesque evidence is to be seen of the craft pursued by some lodger within. Here long poles are hung with immense skeins of dyed worsted put out to dry; there, on ropes, dance clean-washed shirts; higher up, on a shelf, volumes display their freshly marbled edges; women sing, husbands whistle, children shout; the carpenter saws his planks, a copper-turner makes the metal screech; all kinds of industries combine to produce a noise which the number of instruments renders distracting.

The general system of decoration in this passage, which is neither courtyard, garden, nor vaulted way, though a little of all, consists of wooden pillars resting on square stone blocks, and forming arches. Two archways open on to the little garden; two others, facing the front gateway, lead to a wooden staircase, with an iron balustrade that was once a miracle of smith's work, so whimsical are the shapes given to the metal; the worn steps creak under every tread. The entrance to each flat has an architrave dark with dirt, grease, and dust, and outer doors, covered with Utrecht velvet set with brass nails, once gilt, in a diamond pattern. These relics of splendor show that in the time of Louis XIV. the house was the residence of some councillor to the Parlement, some rich priests, or some treasurer of the ecclesiastical revenue. But these vestiges of former luxury bring a smile to the lips by the artless contrast of past and present.

M. Jean-Jules Popinot lived on the first floor of this house, where the gloom, natural to all first floors in Paris houses, was increased by the narrowness of the street. This old tenement was known to all the twelfth arrondissement, on which Providence had bestowed this lawyer, as it gives a beneficent plant to cure or alleviate every malady. Here is a sketch of a man whom the brilliant Marquise d'Espard hoped to fascinate.

M. Popinot, as is seemly for a magistrate, was always dressed in black --a style which contributed to make him ridiculous in the eyes of those who were in the habit of judging everything from a superficial examination. Men who are jealous of maintaining the dignity required by this color ought to devote themselves to constant and minute care of their person; but our dear M. Popinot was incapable of forcing himself to the puritanical cleanliness which black demands. His trousers, always threadbare, looked like camlet--the stuff of which attorneys' gowns are made; and his habitual stoop set them, in time, in such innumerable creases, that in places they were traced with lines, whitish, rusty, or shiny, betraying either sordid avarice, or the most unheeding poverty. His coarse worsted stockings were twisted anyhow in his ill-shaped shoes. His linen had the tawny tinge acquired by long sojourn in a wardrobe, showing that the late lamented Madame Popinot had had a mania for much linen; in the Flemish fashion, perhaps, she had given herself the trouble of a great wash no more than twice a year. The old man's coat and waistcoat were in harmony with his trousers, shoes, stockings, and linen. He always had the luck of his carelessness; for, the first day he put on a new coat, he unfailingly matched it with the rest of his costume by staining it with incredible promptitude. The good man waited till his housekeeper told him that his hat was too shabby before buying a new one. His necktie was always crumpled and starchless, and he never set his dog-eared shirt collar straight after his judge's bands had disordered it. He took no care of his gray hair, and shaved but twice a week. He never wore gloves, and generally kept his hands stuffed into his empty trousers' pockets; the soiled pocket-holes, almost always torn, added a final touch to the slovenliness of his person.

Any one who knows the Palais de Justice at Paris, where every variety of black attire may be studied, can easily imagine the appearance of M. Popinot. The habit of sitting for days at a time modifies the structure of the body, just as the fatigue of hearing interminable pleadings tells on the expression of a magistrate's face. Shut up as he is in courts ridiculously small, devoid of architectural dignity, and where the air is quickly vitiated, a Paris judge inevitably acquires a countenance puckered and seamed by reflection, and depressed by weariness; his complexion turns pallid, acquiring an earthy or greenish hue according to his individual temperament. In short, within a given time the most blooming young man is turned into an "inasmuch" machine--an instrument which applies the Code to individual cases with the indifference of clockwork.

Hence, nature, having bestowed on M. Popinot a not too pleasing exterior, his life as a lawyer had not improved it. His frame was graceless and angular. His thick knees, huge feet, and broad hands formed a contrast with a priest-like face having a vague resemblance to a calf's head, meek to unmeaningness, and but little brightened by divergent bloodless eyes, divided by a straight flat nose, surmounted by a flat forehead, flanked by enormous ears, flabby and graceless. His thin, weak hair showed the baldness through various irregular partings.

One feature only commended this face to the physiognomist. This man had a mouth to whose lips divine kindness lent its sweetness. They were wholesome, full, red lips, finely wrinkled, sinuous, mobile, by which nature had given expression to noble feelings; lips which spoke to the heart and proclaimed the man's intelligence and lucidity, a gift of second-sight, and a heavenly temper; and you would have judged him wrongly from looking merely at his sloping forehead, his fireless eyes, and his shambling gait. His life answered to his countenance; it was full of secret labor, and hid the virtue of a saint. His superior knowledge of law proved so strong a recommendation at a time when Napoleon was reorganizing it in 1808 and 1811, that, by the advice of Cambaceres, he was one of the first men named to sit on the Imperial High Court of Justice at Paris. Popinot was no schemer. Whenever any demand was made, any request preferred for an appointment, the Minister would overlook Popinot, who never set foot in the house of the High Chancellor or the Chief Justice. From the High Court he was sent down to the Common Court, and pushed to the lowest rung of the ladder by active struggling men. There he was appointed supernumerary judge. There was a general outcry among the lawyers: "Popinot a supernumerary!" Such injustice struck the legal world with dismay--the attorneys, the registrars, everybody but Popinot himself, who made no complaint. The first clamor over, everybody was satisfied that all was for the best in the best of all possible worlds, which must certainly be the legal world. Popinot remained supernumerary judge till the day when the most famous Great Seal under the Restoration avenged the oversights heaped on this modest and uncomplaining man by the Chief Justices of the Empire. After being a supernumerary for twelve years, M. Popinot would no doubt die a puisne judge of the Court of the Seine.

To account for the obscure fortunes of one of the superior men of the legal profession, it is necessary to enter here into some details which will serve to reveal his life and character, and which will, at the same time, display some of the wheels of the great machine known as Justice. M. Popinot was classed by the three Presidents who successively controlled the Court of the Seine under the category of possible judges, the stuff of which judges are made. Thus classified, he did not achieve the reputation for capacity which his previous labors had deserved. Just as a painter is invariably included in a category as a landscape painter, a portrait painter, a painter of history, of sea pieces, or of genre, by a public consisting of artists, connoisseurs, and simpletons, who, out of envy, or critical omnipotence, or prejudice, fence in his intellect, assuming, one and all, that there are ganglions in every brain--a narrow judgment which the world applies to writers, to statesmen, to everybody who begins with some specialty before being hailed as omniscient; so Popinot's fate was sealed, and he was hedged round to do a particular kind of work. Magistrates, attorneys, pleaders, all who pasture on the legal common, distinguish two elements in every case--law and equity. Equity is the outcome of facts, law is the application of principles to facts. A man may be right in equity but wrong in law, without any blame to the judge. Between his conscience and the facts there is a whole gulf of determining reasons unknown to the judge, but which condemn or legitimatize the act. A judge is not God; the duty is to adapt facts to principles, to judge cases of infinite variety while measuring them by a fixed standard.

France employs about six thousand judges; no generation has six thousand great men at her command, much less can she find them in the legal profession. Popinot, in the midst of the civilization of Paris, was just a very clever cadi, who, by the character of his mind, and by dint of rubbing the letter of the law into the essence of facts, had learned to see the error of spontaneous and violent decisions. By the help of his judicial second-sight he could pierce the double casing of lies in which advocates hide the heart of a trial. He was a judge, as the great Desplein was a surgeon; he probed men's consciences as the anatomist probed their bodies. His life and habits had led him to an exact appreciation of their most secret thoughts by a thorough study of facts.

He sifted a case as Cuvier sifted the earth's crust. Like that great thinker, he proceeded from deduction to deduction before drawing his conclusions, and reconstructed the past career of a conscience as Cuvier reconstructed an Anoplotherium. When considering a brief he would often wake in the night, startled by a gleam of truth suddenly sparkling in his brain. Struck by the deep injustice, which is the end of these contests, in which everything is against the honest man, everything to the advantage of the rogue, he often summed up in favor of equity against law in such cases as bore on questions of what may be termed divination. Hence he was regarded by his colleagues as a man not of a practical mind; his arguments on two lines of deduction made their deliberations lengthy. When Popinot observed their dislike to listening to him he gave his opinion briefly; it was said that he was not a good judge in this class of cases; but as his gift of discrimination was remarkable, his opinion lucid, and his penetration profound, he was considered to have a special aptitude for the laborious duties of an examining judge. So an examining judge he remained during the greater part of his legal career.

Although his qualifications made him eminently fitted for its difficult functions, and he had the reputation of being so learned in criminal law that his duty was a pleasure to him, the kindness of his heart constantly kept him in torture, and he was nipped as in a vise between his conscience and his pity. The services of an examining judge are better paid than those of a judge in civil actions, but they do not therefore prove a temptation; they are too onerous. Popinot, a man of modest and virtuous learning, without ambition, an indefatigable worker, never complained of his fate; he sacrificed his tastes and his compassionate soul to the public good, and allowed himself to be transported to the noisome pools of criminal examinations, where he showed himself alike severe and beneficent. His clerk sometimes would give the accused some money to buy tobacco, or a warm winter garment, as he led him back from the judge's office to the Souriciere, the mouse-trap--the House of Detention where the accused are kept under the orders of the Examining Judge. He knew how to be an inflexible judge and a charitable man. And no one extracted a confession so easily as he without having recourse to judicial trickery. He had, too, all the acumen of an observer. This man, apparently so foolishly good-natured, simple, and absent-minded, could guess all the cunning of a prison wag, unmask the astutest street huzzy, and subdue a scoundrel. Unusual circumstances had sharpened his perspicacity; but to relate these we must intrude on his domestic history, for in him the judge was the social side of the man; another man, greater and less known, existed within.

Twelve years before the beginning of this story, in 1816, during the terrible scarcity which coincided disastrously with the stay in France of the so-called Allies, Popinot was appointed President of the Commission Extraordinary formed to distribute food to the poor of his neighborhood, just when he had planned to move from the Rue du Fouarre, which he as little liked to live in as his wife did. The great lawyer, the clear-sighted criminal judge, whose superiority seemed to his colleagues a form of aberration, had for five years been watching legal results without seeing their causes. As he scrambled up into the lofts, as he saw the poverty, as he studied the desperate necessities which gradually bring the poor to criminal acts, as he estimated their long struggles, compassion filled his soul. The judge then became the Saint Vincent de Paul of these grown up children, these suffering toilers. The transformation was not immediately complete. Beneficence has its temptations as vice has. Charity consumes a saint's purse, as roulette consumes the possessions of a gambler, quite gradually. Popinot went from misery to misery, from charity to charity; then, by the time he had lifted all the rags which cover public pauperism, like a bandage under which an inflamed wound lies festering, at the end of a year he had become the Providence incarnate of that quarter of the town. He was a member of the Benevolent Committee and of the Charity Organization. Wherever any gratuitous services were needed he was ready, and did everything without fuss, like the man with the short cloak, who spends his life in carrying soup round the markets and other places where there are starving folks.

Popinot was fortunate in acting on a larger circle and in a higher sphere; he had an eye on everything, he prevented crime, he gave work to the unemployed, he found a refuge for the helpless, he distributed aid with discernment wherever danger threatened, he made himself the counselor of the widow, the protector of homeless children, the sleeping partner of small traders. No one at the Courts, no one in Paris, knew of this secret life of Popinot's. There are virtues so splendid that they necessitate obscurity; men make haste to hide them under a bushel. As to those whom the lawyer succored, they, hard at work all day and tired at night, were little able to sing his praises; theirs was the gracelessness of children, who can never pay because they owe too much. There is such compulsory ingratitude; but what heart that has sown good to reap gratitude can think itself great?

By the end of the second year of his apostolic work, Popinot had turned the storeroom at the bottom of his house into a parlor, lighted by the three iron-barred windows. The walls and ceiling of this spacious room were whitewashed, and the furniture consisted of wooden benches like those seen in schools, a clumsy cupboard, a walnut-wood writing-table, and an armchair. In the cupboard were his registers of donations, his tickets for orders for bread, and his diary. He kept his ledger like a tradesman, that he might not be ruined by kindness. All the sorrows of the neighborhood were entered and numbered in a book, where each had its little account, as merchants' customers have theirs. When there was any question as to a man or a family needing help, the lawyer could always command information from the police.

Lavienne, a man made for his master, was his aide-de-camp. He redeemed or renewed pawn-tickets, and visited the districts most threatened with famine, while his master was in court.

From four till seven in the morning in summer, from six till nine in winter, this room was full of women, children, and paupers, while Popinot gave audience. There was no need for a stove in winter; the crowd was so dense that the air was warmed; only, Lavienne strewed straw on the wet floor. By long use the benches were as polished as varnished mahogany; at the height of a man's shoulders the wall had a coat of dark, indescribable color, given to it by the rags and tattered clothes of these poor creatures. The poor wretches loved Popinot so well that when they assembled before his door was opened, before daybreak on a winter's morning, the women warming themselves with their foot-brasiers, the men swinging their arms for circulation, never a sound had disturbed his sleep. Rag-pickers and other toilers of the night knew the house, and often saw a light burning in the lawyer's private room at unholy hours. Even thieves, as they passed by, said, "That is his house," and respected it. The morning he gave to the poor, the mid-day hours to criminals, the evening to law work.

Thus the gift of observation that characterized Popinot was necessarily bifrons; he could guess the virtues of a pauper--good feelings nipped, fine actions in embryo, unrecognized self-sacrifice, just as he could read at the bottom of a man's conscience the faintest outlines of a crime, the slenderest threads of wrongdoing, and infer all the rest.

Popinot's inherited fortune was a thousand crowns a year. His wife, sister to M. Bianchon /Senior/, a doctor at Sancerre, had brought him about twice as much. She, dying five years since, had left her fortune to her husband. As the salary of a supernumerary judge is not large, and Popinot had been a fully salaried judge only for four years, we may guess his reasons for parsimony in all that concerned his person and mode of life, when we consider how small his means were and how great his beneficence. Besides, is not such indifference to dress as stamped Popinot

an absent-minded man, a distinguishing mark of scientific attainment, of art pas-
sionately pursued, of a perpetually active mind? To complete this portrait, it will be
enough to add that Popinot was one of the few judges of the Court of the Seine on
whom the ribbon of the Legion of Honor had not been conferred.

Such was the man who had been instructed by the President of the Second
Chamber of the Court--to which Popinot had belonged since his reinstatement
among the judges in civil law--to examine the Marquis d'Espard at the request of
his wife, who sued for a Commission in Lunacy.

The Rue du Fouarre, where so many unhappy wretches swarmed in the early
morning, would be deserted by nine o'clock, and as gloomy and squalid as ever.
Bianchon put his horse to a trot in order to find his uncle in the midst of his business. It was not without a smile that he thought of the curious contrast the judge's
appearance would make in Madame d'Espard's room; but he promised himself that
he would persuade him to dress in a way that should not be too ridiculous.

"If only my uncle happens to have a new coat!" said Bianchon to himself, as he
turned into the Rue du Fouarre, where a pale light shone from the parlor windows.
"I shall do well, I believe, to talk that over with Lavienne."

At the sound of wheels half a score of startled paupers came out from under
the gateway, and took off their hats on recognizing Bianchon; for the doctor, who
treated gratuitously the sick recommended to him by the lawyer, was not less well
known than he to the poor creatures assembled there.

Bianchon found his uncle in the middle of the parlor, where the benches were
occupied by patients presenting such grotesque singularities of costume as would
have made the least artistic passer-by turn round to gaze at them. A draughtsman--a
Rembrandt, if there were one in our day--might have conceived of one of his fin-
est compositions from seeing these children of misery, in artless attitudes, and all
silent.

Here was the rugged countenance of an old man with a white beard and an
apostolic head--a Saint Peter ready to hand; his chest, partly uncovered, showed
salient muscles, the evidence of an iron constitution which had served him as a
fulcrum to resist a whole poem of sorrows. There a young woman was suckling her
youngest-born to keep it from crying, while another of about five stood between
her knees. Her white bosom, gleaming amid rags, the baby with its transparent

flesh-tints, and the brother, whose attitude promised a street arab in the future, touched the fancy with pathos by its almost graceful contrast with the long row of faces crimson with cold, in the midst of which sat this family group. Further away, an old woman, pale and rigid, had the repulsive look of rebellious pauperism, eager to avenge all its past woes in one day of violence.

There, again, was the young workman, weakly and indolent, whose brightly intelligent eye revealed fine faculties crushed by necessity struggled with in vain, saying nothing of his sufferings, and nearly dead for lack of an opportunity to squeeze between the bars of the vast stews where the wretched swim round and round and devour each other.

The majority were women; their husbands, gone to their work, left it to them, no doubt, to plead the cause of the family with the ingenuity which characterizes the woman of the people, who is almost always queen in her hovel. You would have seen a torn bandana on every head, on every form a skirt deep in mud, ragged kerchiefs, worn and dirty jackets, but eyes that burnt like live coals. It was a horrible assemblage, raising at first sight a feeling of disgust, but giving a certain sense of terror the instant you perceived that the resignation of these souls, all engaged in the struggle for every necessary of life, was purely fortuitous, a speculation on benevolence. The two tallow candles which lighted the parlor flickered in a sort of fog caused by the fetid atmosphere of the ill-ventilated room.

The magistrate himself was not the least picturesque figure in the midst of this assembly. He had on his head a rusty cotton night-cap; as he had no cravat, his neck was visible, red with cold and wrinkled, in contrast with the threadbare collar of his old dressing-gown. His worn face had the half-stupid look that comes of absorbed attention. His lips, like those of all men who work, were puckered up like a bag with the strings drawn tight. His knitted brows seemed to bear the burden of all the sorrows confided to him: he felt, analyzed, and judged them all. As watchful as a Jew money-lender, he never raised his eyes from his books and registers but to look into the very heart of the persons he was examining, with the flashing glance by which a miser expresses his alarm.

Lavienne, standing behind his master, ready to carry out his orders, served no doubt as a sort of police, and welcomed newcomers by encouraging them to get over their shyness. When the doctor appeared there was a stir on the benches. Lavienne turned his head, and was strangely surprised to see Bianchon.

"Ah! It is you, old boy!" exclaimed Popinot, stretching himself. "What brings you so early?"

"I was afraid lest you should make an official visit about which I wish to speak to you before I could see you."

"Well," said the lawyer, addressing a stout little woman who was still standing close to him, "if you do not tell me what it is you want, I cannot guess it, child."

"Make haste," said Lavienne. "Do not waste other people's time."

"Monsieur," said the woman at last, turning red, and speaking so low as only to be heard by Popinot and Lavienne, "I have a green-grocery truck, and I have my last baby to nurse, and I owe for his keep. Well, I had hidden my little bit of money----"

"Yes; and your man took it?" said Popinot, guessing the sequel.

"Yes, sir."

"What is your name?"

"La Pomponne."

"And your husband's?"

"Toupinet."

"Rue du Petit-Banquier?" said Popinot, turning over his register. "He is in prison," he added, reading a note at the margin of the section in which this family was described.

"For debt, my kind monsieur."

Popinot shook his head.

"But I have nothing to buy any stock for my truck; the landlord came yesterday and made me pay up; otherwise I should have been turned out."

Lavienne bent over his master, and whispered in his ear.

"Well, how much do you want to buy fruit in the market?"

"Why, my good monsieur, to carry on my business, I should want--Yes, I should certainly want ten francs."

Popinot signed to Lavienne, who took ten francs out of a large bag, and handed them to the woman, while the lawyer made a note of the loan in his ledger. As he saw the thrill of delight that made the poor hawker tremble, Bianchon understood the apprehensions that must have agitated her on her way to the lawyer's house.

"You next," said Lavienne to the old man with the white beard.

Bianchon drew the servant aside, and asked him how long this audience would last.

"Monsieur has had two hundred persons this morning, and there are eight to be turned off," said Lavienne. "You will have time to pay your early visit, sir."

"Here, my boy," said the lawyer, turning round and taking Horace by the arm; "here are two addresses near this--one in the Rue de Seine, and the other in the Rue de l'Arbalete. Go there at once. Rue de Seine, a young girl has just asphyxiated herself; and Rue de l'Arbalete, you will find a man to remove to your hospital. I will wait breakfast for you."

Bianchon returned an hour later. The Rue du Fouarre was deserted; day was beginning to dawn there; his uncle had gone up to his rooms; the last poor wretch whose misery the judge had relieved was departing, and Lavienne's money bag was empty.

"Well, how are they going on?" asked the old lawyer, as the doctor came in.

"The man is dead," replied Bianchon; "the girl will get over it."

Since the eye and hand of a woman had been lacking, the flat in which Popinot lived had assumed an aspect in harmony with its master's. The indifference of a man who is absorbed in one dominant idea had set its stamp of eccentricity on everything. Everywhere lay unconquerable dust, every object was adapted to a wrong purpose with a pertinacity suggestive of a bachelor's home. There were papers in the flower vases, empty ink-bottles on the tables, plates that had been forgotten, matches used as tapers for a minute when something had to be found, drawers or boxes half-turned out and left unfinished; in short, all the confusion and vacancies resulting from plans for order never carried out. The lawyer's private room, especially disordered by this incessant rummage, bore witness to his unresting pace, the hurry of a man overwhelmed with business, hunted by contradictory necessities. The bookcase looked as if it had been sacked; there were books scattered over everything, some piled up open, one on another, others on the floor face downwards; registers of proceedings laid on the floor in rows, lengthwise, in front of the shelves; and that floor had not been polished for two years.

The tables and shelves were covered with ex votos, the offerings of the grateful poor. On a pair of blue glass jars which ornamented the chimney-shelf there were two glass balls, of which the core was made up of many-colored fragments, giving them the appearance of some singular natural product. Against the wall hung frames of artificial flowers, and decorations in which Popinot's initials were surrounded by hearts and everlasting flowers. Here were boxes of elaborate and useless cabinet work; there letter-weights carved in the style of work done by convicts in penal servitude. These masterpieces of patience, enigmas of gratitude, and withered bouquets gave the lawyer's room the appearance of a toyshop. The good man used these works of art as hiding-places which he filled with bills, worn-out pens, and scraps of paper. All these pathetic witnesses to his divine charity were thick with dust, dingy, and faded.

Some birds, beautifully stuffed, but eaten by moth, perched in this wilderness of trumpery, presided over by an Angora cat, Madame Popinot's pet, restored to her no doubt with all the graces of life by some impecunious naturalist, who thus repaid a gift of charity with a perennial treasure. Some local artist whose heart had misguided his brush had painted portraits of M. and Madame Popinot. Even in the bedroom there were embroidered pin-cushions, landscapes in cross-stitch, and crosses in folded paper, so elaborately cockled as to show the senseless labor they had cost.

The window-curtains were black with smoke, and the hangings absolutely colorless. Between the fireplace and the large square table at which the magistrate worked, the cook had set two cups of coffee on a small table, and two armchairs, in mahogany and horsehair, awaited the uncle and nephew. As daylight, darkened by the windows, could not penetrate to this corner, the cook had left two dips burning, whose unsnuffed wicks showed a sort of mushroom growth, giving the red light which promises length of life to the candle from slowness of combustion--a discovery due to some miser.

"My dear uncle, you ought to wrap yourself more warmly when you go down to that parlor."

"I cannot bear to keep them waiting, poor souls!--Well, and what do you want of me?"

"I have come to ask you to dine to-morrow with the Marquise d'Espard."

"A relation of ours?" asked Popinot, with such genuine absence of mind that Bianchon laughed.

"No, uncle; the Marquise d'Espard is a high and puissant lady, who has laid before the Courts a petition desiring that a Commission in Lunacy should sit on her husband, and you are appointed----"

"And you want me to dine with her! Are you mad?" said the lawyer, taking up the code of proceedings. "Here, only read this article, prohibiting any magistrate's eating or drinking in the house of either of two parties whom he is called upon to decide between. Let her come and see me, your Marquise, if she has anything to say to me. I was, in fact, to go to examine her husband to-morrow, after working the case up to-night."

He rose, took up a packet of papers that lay under a weight where he could see it, and after reading the title, he said:

"Here is the affidavit. Since you take an interest in this high and puissant lady, let us see what she wants."

Popinot wrapped his dressing-gown across his body, from which it was constantly slipping and leaving his chest bare; he sopped his bread in the half-cold coffee, and opened the petition, which he read, allowing himself to throw in a parenthesis now and then, and some discussions, in which his nephew took part:--

"'To Monsieur the President of the Civil Tribunal of the Lower Court of the Department of the Seine, sitting at the Palais de Justice.

"'Madame Jeanne Clementine Athenais de Blamont-Chauvry, wife of M. Charles Maurice Marie Andoche, Comte de Negrepelisse, Marquis d'Espard'--a very good family--'landowner, the said Mme. d'Espard living in the Rue du Faubourg Saint-Honore, No. 104, and the said M. d'Espard in the Rue de la Montagne-Sainte-Genevieve, No. 22,'--to be sure, the President told me he lived in this part of the town--'having for her solicitor Maitre Desroches'--Desroches! a pettifogging jobber, a man looked down upon by his brother lawyers, and who does his clients no good--"

"Poor fellow!" said Bianchon, "unluckily he has no money, and he rushes round like the devil in holy water--That is all."

"'Has the honor to submit to you, Monsieur the President, that for a year past the moral and intellectual powers of her husband, M. d'Espard, have undergone so serious a change, that at the present day they have reached the state of dementia and idiocy provided for by Article 448 of the Civil Code, and require the application of the remedies set forth by that article, for the security of his fortune and his person, and to guard the interest of his children whom he keeps to live with him.

"'That, in point of fact, the mental condition of M. d'Espard, which for some years has given grounds for alarm based on the system he has pursued in the management of his affairs, has reached, during the last twelvemonth, a deplorable depth of depression; that his infirm will was the first thing to show the results of the malady; and that its effete state leaves M. the Marquis d'Espard exposed to all the perils of his incompetency, as is proved by the following facts:

"'For a long time all the income accruing from M. d'Espard's estates are paid, without any reasonable cause, or even temporary advantage, into the hands of an old woman, whose repulsive ugliness is generally remarked on, named Madame Jeanrenaud, living sometimes in Paris, Rue de la Vrilliere, No. 8, sometimes at Villeparisis, near Claye, in the Department of Seine et Marne, and for the benefit of her son, aged thirty-six, an officer in the ex-Imperial Guards, whom the Marquis d'Espard has placed by his influence in the King's Guards, as Major in the First Regiment of Cuirassiers. These two persons, who in 1814 were in extreme poverty, have since then purchased house-property of considerable value; among other items, quite recently, a large house in the Grand Rue Verte, where the said Jeanrenaud is laying out considerable sums in order to settle there with the woman Jeanrenaud, intending to marry: these sums amount already to more than a hundred thousand francs. The marriage has been arranged by the intervention of M. d'Espard with his banker, one Mongenod, whose niece he has asked in marriage for the said Jeanrenaud, promising to use his influence to procure him the title and dignity of baron. This has in fact been secured by His Majesty's letters patent, dated December 29th of last year, at the request of the Marquis d'Espard, as can be proved by His Excellency the Keeper of the Seals, if the Court should think proper to require his testimony.

"'That no reason, not even such as morality and the law would concur in disapproving, can justify the influence which the said Mme. Jeanrenaud exerts over M. d'Espard, who, indeed, sees her very seldom; nor account for his strange affection for the said Baron Jeanrenaud, Major with whom he has but little intercourse. And yet their power is so considerable, that whenever they need money, if only to gratify a mere whim, this lady, or her son----' Heh, heh! /No reason even such as morality and the law concur in disapproving!/ What does the clerk or the attorney mean to insinuate?" said Popinot.

Bianchon laughed.

"'This lady, or her son, obtain whatever they ask of the Marquis d'Espard without demur; and if he has not ready money, M. d'Espard draws bills to be paid by the said Mongenod, who has offered to give evidence to that effect for the petitioner.

"'That, moreover, in further proof of these facts, lately, on the occasion of the renewal of the leases on the Espard estate, the farmers having paid a considerable premium for the renewal of their leases on the old terms, M. Jeanrenaud at once secured the payment of it into his own hands.

"'That the Marquis d'Espard parts with these sums of money so little of his own free-will, that when he was spoken to on the subject he seemed to remember nothing of the matter; that whenever anybody of any weight has questioned him as to his devotion to these two persons, his replies have shown so complete an absence of ideas and of sense of his own interests, that there obviously must be some occult cause at work to which the petitioner begs to direct the eye of justice, inasmuch as it is impossible but that this cause should be criminal, malignant, and wrongful, or else of a nature to come under medical jurisdiction; unless this influence is of the kind which constitutes an abuse of moral power--such as can only be described by the word /possession/ ----'The devil!" exclaimed Popinot. "What do you say to that, doctor. These are strange statements."

"They might certainly," said Bianchon, "be an effect of magnetic force."

"Then do you believe in Mesmer's nonsense, and his tub, and seeing through walls?"

"Yes, uncle," said the doctor gravely. "As I heard you read that petition I thought of that. I assure you that I have verified, in another sphere of action, several analogous facts proving the unlimited influence one man may acquire over another. In contradiction to the opinion of my brethren, I am perfectly convinced of the power of the will regarded as a motor force. All collusion and charlatanism apart, I have seen the results of such a possession. Actions promised during sleep by a magnetized patient to the magnetizer have been scrupulously performed on waking. The will of one had become the will of the other."

"Every kind of action?"

"Yes."

"Even a criminal act?"

"Even a crime."

"If it were not from you, I would not listen to such a thing."

"I will make you witness it," said Bianchon.

"Hm, hm," muttered the lawyer. "But supposing that this so-called possession fell under this class of facts, it would be difficult to prove it as legal evidence."

"If this woman Jeanrenaud is so hideously old and ugly, I do not see what other means of fascination she can have used," observed Bianchon.

"But," observed the lawyer, "in 1814, the time at which this fascination is supposed to have taken place, this woman was fourteen years younger; if she had been connected with M. d'Espard ten years before that, these calculations take us back four-and-twenty years, to a time when the lady may have been young and pretty, and have won for herself and her son a power over M. d'Espard which some men do not know how to evade. Though the source of this power is reprehensible in the sight of justice, it is justifiable in the eye of nature. Madame Jeanrenaud may have been aggrieved by the marriage, contracted probably at about that time, between the Marquis d'Espard and Mademoiselle de Blamont-Chauvry, and at the bottom of all this there may be nothing more than the rivalry of two women, since the Marquis had for a long time lived apart from Mme. d'Espard."

"But her repulsive ugliness, uncle?"

"Power of fascination is in direct proportion to ugliness," said the lawyer; "that is the old story. And then think of the smallpox, doctor. But to proceed.

"'That so long ago as in 1815, in order to supply the sums of money required by these two persons, the Marquis d'Espard went with his two children to live in the Rue de la Montagne-Sainte-Genevieve, in rooms quite unworthy of his name and rank'--well, we may live as we please --'that he keeps his two children there, the Comte Clement d'Espard and Vicomte Camille d'Espard, in a style of living quite unsuited to their future prospects, their name and fortune; that he often wants money, to such a point, that not long since the landlord, one Mariast, put in an execution on the furniture in the rooms; that when this execution was carried out in his presence, the Marquis d'Espard helped the bailiff, whom he treated like a man of rank, paying him all the marks of attention and respect which he would have shown to a person of superior birth and dignity to himself.'"

The uncle and nephew glanced at each other and laughed.

"'That, moreover, every act of his life, besides the facts with reference to the widow Jeanrenaud and the Baron Jeanrenaud, her son, are those of a madman; that for nearly ten years he has given his thoughts exclusively to China, its customs, manners, and history; that he refers everything to a Chinese origin; that when he is questioned on the subject, he confuses the events of the day and the business of yesterday with facts relating to China; that he censures the acts of the Government and the conduct of the King, though he is personally much attached to him, by comparing them with the politics of China;

"'That this monomania has driven the Marquis d'Espard to conduct devoid of all sense: against the customs of men of rank, and, in opposition to his own professed ideas as to the duties of the nobility, he has joined a commercial undertaking, for which he constantly draws bills which, as they fall due, threaten both his honor and his fortune, since they stamp him as a trader, and in default of payment may lead to his being declared insolvent; that these debts, which are owing to stationers, printers, lithographers, and print-colorists, who have supplied the materials for his publication, called A Picturesque History of China, now coming out in parts, are so heavy that these tradesmen have requested the petitioner to apply for a Commission in Lunacy with regard to the Marquis d'Espard in order to save their own credit.'"

"The man is mad!" exclaimed Bianchon.

"You think so, do you?" said his uncle. "If you listen to only one bell, you hear only one sound."

"But it seems to me----" said Bianchon.

"But it seems to me," said Popinot, "that if any relation of mine wanted to get hold of the management of my affairs, and if, instead of being a humble lawyer, whose colleagues can, any day, verify what his condition is, I were a duke of the realm, an attorney with a little cunning, like Desroches, might bring just such a petition against me.

"'That his children's education has been neglected for this monomania; and that he has taught them, against all the rules of education, the facts of Chinese history, which contradict the tenets of the Catholic Church. He also has them taught the Chinese dialects.'"

"Here Desroches strikes me as funny," said Bianchon.

"The petition is drawn up by his head-clerk Godeschal, who, as you know, is not strong in Chinese," said the lawyer.

"'That he often leaves his children destitute of the most necessary things; that the petitioner, notwithstanding her entreaties, can never see them; that the said Marquis d'Espard brings them to her only once a year; that, knowing the privations to which they are exposed, she makes vain efforts to give them the things most necessary for their existence, and which they require----' Oh! Madame la Marquise, this is preposterous. By proving too much you prove nothing.--My dear boy," said the old man, laying the document on his knee, "where is the mother who ever lacked heart and wit and yearning to such a degree as to fall below the inspirations suggested by her animal instinct? A mother is as cunning to get at her children as a girl can be in the conduct of a love intrigue. If your Marquise really wanted to give her children food and clothes, the Devil himself would not have hindered her, heh? That is rather too big a fable for an old lawyer to swallow! --To proceed.

"'That at the age the said children have now attained it is necessary that steps should be taken to preserve them from the evil effects of such an education; that they should be provided for as beseems their rank, and that they should cease to have before their eyes the sad example of their father's conduct;

"'That there are proofs in support of these allegations which the Court can easily order to be produced. Many times has M. d'Espard spoken of the judge of the Twelfth Arrondissement as a mandarin of the third class; he often speaks of the professors of the College Henri IV. as "men of letters"'--and that offends them! 'In speaking of the simplest things, he says, "They were not done so in China;" in the course of the most ordinary conversation he will sometimes allude to Madame Jeanrenaud, or sometimes to events which happened in the time of Louis XIV., and then sit plunged in the darkest melancholy; sometimes he fancies he is in China. Several of his neighbors, among others one Edme Becker, medical student, and Jean Baptiste Fremiot, a professor, living under the same roof, are of opinion, after frequent intercourse with the Marquis d'Espard, that his monomania with regard to everything Chinese is the result of a scheme laid by the said Baron Jeanrenaud and the widow his mother to bring about the deadening of all the Marquis d'Espard's mental faculties, since the only service which Mme. Jeanrenaud appears to render

M. d'Espard is to procure him everything that relates to the Chinese Empire;

"'Finally, that the petitioner is prepared to show to the Court that the moneys absorbed by the said Baron and Mme. Jeanrenaud between 1814 and 1828 amount to not less than one million francs.

"'In confirmation of the facts herein set forth, the petitioner can bring the evidence of persons who are in the habit of seeing the Marquis d'Espard, whose names and professions are subjoined, many of whom have urged her to demand a commission in lunacy to declare M. d'Espard incapable of managing his own affairs, as being the only way to preserve his fortune from the effects of his maladministration and his children from his fatal influence.

"'Taking all this into consideration, M. le President, and the affidavits subjoined, the petitioner desires that it may please you, inasmuch as the foregoing facts sufficiently prove the insanity and incompetency of the Marquis d'Espard herein described with his titles and residence, to order that, to the end that he may be declared incompetent by law, this petition and the documents in evidence may be laid before the King's public prosecutor; and that you will charge one of the judges of this Court to make his report to you on any day you may be pleased to name, and thereupon to pronounce judgment,' etc.

"And here," said Popinot, "is the President's order instructing me! --Well, what does the Marquise d'Espard want with me? I know everything. But I shall go tomorrow with my registrar to see M. le Marquis, for this does not seem at all clear to me."

"Listen, my dear uncle, I have never asked the least little favor of you that had to do with your legal functions; well, now I beg you to show Madame d'Espard the kindness which her situation deserves. If she came here, you would listen to her?"

"Yes."

"Well, then, go and listen to her in her own house. Madame d'Espard is a sickly, nervous, delicate woman, who would faint in your rat-hole of a place. Go in the evening, instead of accepting her dinner, since the law forbids your eating or drinking at your client's expense."

"And does not the law forbid you from taking any legacy from your dead?" said Popinot, fancying that he saw a touch of irony on his nephew's lips.

"Come, uncle, if it were only to enable you to get at the truth of this business, grant my request. You will come as the examining judge, since matters do not seem to you very clear. Deuce take it! It is as necessary to cross-question the Marquise as it is to examine the Marquis."

"You are right," said the lawyer. "It is quite possible that it is she who is mad. I will go."

"I will call for you. Write down in your engagement book: 'To-morrow evening at nine, Madame d'Espard.'--Good!" said Bianchon, seeing his uncle make a note of the engagement.

Next evening at nine Bianchon mounted his uncle's dusty staircase, and found him at work on the statement of some complicated judgment. The coat Lavienne had ordered of the tailor had not been sent, so Popinot put on his old stained coat, and was the Popinot unadorned whose appearance made those laugh who did not know the secrets of his private life. Bianchon, however, obtained permission to pull his cravat straight, and to button his coat, and he hid the stains by crossing the breast of it with the right side over the left, and so displaying the new front of the cloth. But in a minute the judge rucked the coat up over his chest by the way in which he stuffed his hands into his pockets, obeying an irresistible habit. Thus the coat, deeply wrinkled both in front and behind, made a sort of hump in the middle of the back, leaving a gap between the waistcoat and trousers through which his shirt showed. Bianchon, to his sorrow, only discovered this crowning absurdity at the moment when his uncle entered the Marquise's room.

A brief sketch of the person and the career of the lady in whose presence the doctor and the judge now found themselves is necessary for an understanding of her interview with Popinot.

Madame d'Espard had, for the last seven years, been very much the fashion in Paris, where Fashion can raise and drop by turns various personages who, now great and now small, that is to say, in view or forgotten, are at last quite intolerable--as discarded ministers are, and every kind of decayed sovereignty. These flatterers of the past, odious with their stale pretensions, know everything, speak ill of everything, and, like ruined profligates, are friends with all the world. Since her husband had separated from her in 1815, Madame d'Espard must have married in the beginning of 1812. Her children, therefore, were aged respectively fifteen and thirteen. By what luck was the mother of a family, about three-and-thirty years of age, still the fashion?

Though Fashion is capricious, and no one can foresee who shall be her favorites, though she often exalts a banker's wife, or some woman of very doubtful elegance and beauty, it certainly seems supernatural when Fashion puts on constitutional airs and gives promotion for age. But in this case Fashion had done as the world did, and accepted Madame d'Espard as still young.

The Marquise, who was thirty-three by her register of birth, was twenty-two in a drawing-room in the evening. But by what care, what artifice! Elaborate curls shaded her temples. She condemned herself to live in twilight, affecting illness so as to sit under the protecting tones of light filtered through muslin. Like Diane de Poitiers, she used cold water in her bath, and, like her again, the Marquise slept on a horse-hair mattress, with morocco-covered pillows to preserve her hair; she ate very little, only drank water, and observed monastic regularity in the smallest actions of her life.

This severe system has, it is said, been carried so far as to the use of ice instead of water, and nothing but cold food, by a famous Polish lady of our day who spends a life, now verging on a century old, after the fashion of a town belle. Fated to live as long as Marion Delorme, whom history has credited with surviving to be a hundred and thirty, the old vice-queen of Poland, at the age of nearly a hundred, has the heart and brain of youth, a charming face, an elegant shape; and in her conversation, sparkling with brilliancy like faggots in the fire, she can compare the men and books of our literature with the men and books of the eighteenth century. Living in Warsaw, she orders her caps of Herbault in Paris. She is a great lady with the amiability of a mere girl; she swims, she runs like a schoolboy, and can sink on to a sofa with the grace of a young coquette; she mocks at death, and laughs at life. After having astonished the Emperor Alexander, she can still amaze the Emperor Nicholas by the splendor of her entertainments. She can still bring tears to the eyes of a youthful lover, for her age is whatever she pleases, and she has the exquisite self-devotion of a grisette. In short, she is herself a fairy tale, unless, indeed, she is a fairy.

Had Madame d'Espard known Madame Zayonseck? Did she mean to imitate her career? Be that as it may, the Marquise proved the merits of the treatment; her complexion was clear, her brow unwrinkled, her figure, like that of Henri II.'s lady-love, preserved the litheness, the freshness, the covered charms which bring a woman love and keep it alive. The simple precautions of this course, suggested by art and nature, and perhaps by experience, had met in her with a general system which confirmed the results. The Marquise was absolutely indifferent to everything that was not herself: men amused her, but no man had ever caused her those deep agitations which stir both natures to their depths, and wreck one on the other. She knew neither hatred nor love. When she was offended, she avenged herself coldly, quietly, at her leisure, waiting for the opportunity to gratify the ill-will she cherished against anybody who dwelt in her unfavorable remembrance. She made no fuss, she did not excite herself, she talked, because she knew that by two words a woman may cause the death of three men.

She had parted from M. d'Espard with the greatest satisfaction. Had he not taken with him two children who at present were troublesome, and in the future would stand in the way of her pretensions? Her most intimate friends, as much as her least persistent admirers, seeing about her none of Cornelia's jewels, who come and go, and unconsciously betray their mother's age, took her for quite a young woman. The two boys, about whom she seemed so anxious in her petition, were, like their father, as unknown in the world as the northwest passage is unknown to navigators. M. d'Espard was supposed to be an eccentric personage who had deserted his wife without having the smallest cause for complaint against her.

Mistress of herself at two-and-twenty, and mistress of her fortune of twenty-six thousand francs a year, the Marquise hesitated long before deciding on a course of action and ordering her life. Though she benefited by the expenses her husband had incurred in his house, though she had all the furniture, the carriages, the horses, in short, all the details of a handsome establishment, she lived a retired life during the years 1816, 17, and 18, a time when families were recovering from the disasters resulting from political tempests. She belonged to one of the most important and illustrious families of the Faubourg Saint-Germain, and her parents advised her to live with them as much as possible after the separation forced upon her by her husband's inexplicable caprice.

In 1820 the Marquise roused herself from her lethargy; she went to Court, appeared at parties, and entertained in her own house. From 1821 to 1827 she lived in great style, and made herself remarked for her taste and her dress; she had a day, an hour, for receiving visits, and ere long she had seated herself on the throne, occu-pied before her by Madame la Vicomtesse de Beauseant, the Duchesse de Langeais, and Madame Firmiani--who on her marriage with M. de Camps had resigned the sceptre in favor of the Duchesse de Maufrigneuse, from whom Madame d'Espard snatched it. The world knew nothing beyond this of the private live of the Marquise d'Espard. She seemed likely to shine for long on the Parisian horizon, like the sun near its setting, but which will never set.

The Marquise was on terms of great intimacy with a duchess as famous for her beauty as for her attachment to a prince just now in banishment, but accustomed to play a leading part in every prospective government. Madame d'Espard was also a friend of a foreign lady, with whom a famous and very wily Russian diplomate was in the habit of discussing public affairs. And then an antiquated countess, who was accustomed to shuffle the cards for the great game of politics, had adopted her in a maternal fashion. Thus, to any man of high ambitions, Madame d'Espard was pre-paring a covert but very real influence to follow the public and frivolous ascendency she now owed to fashion. Her drawing-room was acquiring political individuality: "What do they say at Madame d'Espard's?" "Are they against the measure in Ma-dame d'Espard's drawing-room?" were questions repeated by a sufficient number of simpletons to give the flock of the faithful who surrounded her the importance of a coterie. A few damaged politicians whose wounds she had bound up, and whom she flattered, pronounced her as capable in diplomacy as the wife of the Russian ambas-sador to London. The Marquise had indeed several times suggested to deputies or to peers words and ideas that had rung through Europe. She had often judged correctly of certain events on which her circle of friends dared not express an opinion. The principal persons about the Court came in the evening to play whist in her rooms.

Then she also had the qualities of her defects; she was thought to be --and she was--indiscreet. Her friendship seemed to be staunch; she worked for her proteges with a persistency which showed that she cared less for patronage than for increased influence. This conduct was based on her dominant passion, Vanity. Conquests and pleasure, which so many women love, to her seemed only means to an end; she aimed at living on every point of the largest circle that life can describe.

Among the men still young, and to whom the future belonged, who crowd-ed her drawing-room on great occasions, were to be seen MM. de Marsay and de

Ronquerolles, de Montriveau, de la Roche-Hugon, de Serizy, Ferraud, Maxime de Trailles, de Listomere, the two Vandenesses, du Chatelet, and others. She would frequently receive a man whose wife she would not admit, and her power was great enough to induce certain ambitious men to submit to these hard conditions, such as two famous royalist bankers, M. de Nucingen and Ferdinand du Tillet. She had so thoroughly studied the strength and the weakness of Paris life, that her conduct had never given any man the smallest advantage over her. An enormous price might have been set on a note or letter by which she might have compromised herself, without one being produced.

If an arid soul enabled her to play her part to the life, her person was no less available for it. She had a youthful figure. Her voice was, at will, soft and fresh, or clear and hard. She possessed in the highest degree the secret of that aristocratic pose by which a woman wipes out the past. The Marquise knew well the art of setting an immense space between herself and the sort of man who fancies he may be familiar after some chance advances. Her imposing gaze could deny everything. In her conversation fine and beautiful sentiments and noble resolutions flowed naturally, as it seemed, from a pure heart and soul; but in reality she was all self, and quite capable of blasting a man who was clumsy in his negotiations, at the very time when she was shamelessly making a compromise for the benefit of her own interest.

Rastignac, in trying to fasten on to this woman, had discerned her to be the cleverest of tools, but he had not yet used it; far from handling it, he was already finding himself crushed by it. This young Condottiere of the brain, condemned, like Napoleon, to give battle constantly, while knowing that a single defeat would prove the grave of his fortunes, had met a dangerous adversary in his protectress. For the first time in his turbulent life, he was playing a game with a partner worthy of him. He saw a place as Minister in the conquest of Madame d'Espard, so he was her tool till he could make her his--a perilous beginning.

The Hotel d'Espard needed a large household, and the Marquise had a great number of servants. The grand receptions were held in the ground-floor rooms, but she lived on the first floor of the house. The perfect order of a fine staircase splendidly decorated, and rooms fitted in the dignified style which formerly prevailed at Versailles, spoke of an immense fortune. When the judge saw the carriage gates thrown open to admit his nephew's cab, he took in with a rapid glance the lodge, the porter, the courtyard, the stables, the arrangement of the house, the flowers that decorated the stairs, the perfect cleanliness of the banisters, walls, and carpets, and counted the footmen in livery who, as the bell rang, appeared on the landing. His eyes, which only yesterday in his parlor had sounded the dignity of misery under the muddy clothing of the poor, now studied with the same penetrating vision the furniture and splendor of the rooms he passed through, to pierce the misery of grandeur.

"M. Popinot--M. Bianchon."

The two names were pronounced at the door of the boudoir where the Marquise was sitting, a pretty room recently refurnished, and looking out on the garden behind the house. At the moment Madame d'Espard was seated in one of the old rococo armchairs of which Madame had set the fashion. Rastignac was at her left hand on a low chair, in which he looked settled like an Italian lady's "cousin." A third person was standing by the corner of the chimney-piece. As the shrewd doctor had suspected, the Marquise was a woman of a parched and wiry constitution. But for her regimen her complexion must have taken the ruddy tone that is produced by constant heat; but she added to the effect of her acquired pallor by the strong colors of the stuffs she hung her rooms with, or in which she dressed. Reddish-brown, marone, bistre with a golden light in it, suited her to perfection. Her boudoir, copied from that of a famous lady then at the height of fashion in London, was in tan-colored velvet; but she had added various details of ornament which moderated the pompous splendor of this royal hue. Her hair was dressed like a girl's in bands ending in curls, which emphasized the rather long oval of her face; but an oval face is as majestic as a round one is ignoble. The mirrors, cut with facets to lengthen or flatten the face at will, amply proved the rule as applied to the physiognomy.

On seeing Popinot, who stood in the doorway craning his neck like a startled animal, with his left hand in his pocket, and the right hand holding a hat with a greasy lining, the Marquise gave Rastignac a look wherein lay a germ of mockery. The good man's rather foolish appearance was so completely in harmony with his grotesque figure and scared looks, that Rastignac, catching sight of Bianchon's dejected expression of humiliation through his uncle, could not help laughing, and turned away. The Marquise bowed a greeting, and made a great effort to rise from her seat, falling back again, not without grace, with an air of apologizing for her incivility by affected weakness.

At this instant the person who was standing between the fireplace and the door bowed slightly, and pushed forward two chairs, which he offered by a gesture to the doctor and the judge; then, when they had seated themselves, he leaned against the wall again, crossing his arms.

A word as to this man. There is living now, in our day, a painter --Decamps--who possesses in the very highest degree the art of commanding your interest in everything he sets before your eyes, whether it be a stone or a man. In this respect his pencil is more skilful than his brush. He will sketch an empty room and leave a broom against the wall. If he chooses, you shall shudder; you shall believe that this broom has just been the instrument of crime, and is dripping with blood; it shall be the broom which the widow Bancal used to clean out the room where Fualdes was murdered. Yes, the painter will touzle that broom like a man in a rage; he will make each hair of it stand on-end as though it were on your own bristling scalp; he will make it the interpreter between the secret poem of his imagination and the poem that shall have its birth in yours. After terrifying you by the aspect of that broom, to-morrow he will draw another, and lying by it a cat, asleep, but mysterious in its sleep, shall tell you that this broom is that on which the wife of a German cobbler rides off to the Sabbath on the Brocken. Or it will be a quite harmless broom, on which he will hang the coat of a clerk in the Treasury. Decamps had in his brush what Paganini had in his bow--a magnetically communicative power.

Well, I should have to transfer to my style that striking genius, that marvelous knack of the pencil, to depict the upright, tall, lean man dressed in black, with black hair, who stood there without speaking a word. This gentleman had a face like a knife-blade, cold and harsh, with a color like Seine water when it was muddy and strewn with fragments of charcoal from a sunken barge. He looked at the floor, listening and passing judgment. His attitude was terrifying. He stood there like the dreadful broom to which Decamps has given the power of revealing a crime. Now and then, in the course of conversation, the Marquise tried to get some tacit advice; but however eager her questioning, he was as grave and as rigid as the statue of the Commendatore.

The worthy Popinot, sitting on the edge of his chair in front of the fire, his hat between his knees, stared at the gilt chandeliers, the clock, and the curiosities with which the chimney-shelf was covered, the velvet and trimmings of the curtains, and all the costly and elegant nothings that a woman of fashion collects about her. He was roused from his homely meditations by Madame d'Espard, who addressed him in a piping tone:

"Monsieur, I owe you a million thanks----"

"A million thanks," thought he to himself, "that is too many; it does not mean one."

"For the trouble you condescend----"

"Condescend!" thought he; "she is laughing at me."

"To take in coming to see an unhappy client, who is too ill to go out----"

Here the lawyer cut the Marquise short by giving her an inquisitorial look, examining the sanitary condition of the unhappy client.

"As sound as a bell," said he to himself.

"Madame," said he, assuming a respectful mien, "you owe me nothing. Although my visit to you is not in strict accordance with the practice of the Court, we ought to spare no pains to discover the truth in cases of this kind. Our judgment is then guided less by the letter of the law than by the promptings of our conscience. Whether I seek the truth here or in my own consulting-room, so long as I find it, all will be well."

While Popinot was speaking, Rastignac was shaking hands with Bianchon; the Marquise welcomed the doctor with a little bow full of gracious significance.

"Who is that?" asked Bianchon in a whisper of Rastignac, indicating the dark man.

"The Chevalier d'Espard, the Marquis' brother."

"Your nephew told me," said the Marquise to Popinot, "how much you are occupied, and I know too that you are so good as to wish to conceal your kind actions, so as to release those whom you oblige from the burden of gratitude. The work in Court is most fatiguing, it would seem. Why have they not twice as many judges?"

"Ah, madame, that would not be difficult; we should be none the worse if they had. But when that happens, fowls will cut their teeth!"

As he heard this speech, so entirely in character with the lawyer's appearance, the Chevalier measured him from head to foot, out of one eye, as much as to say, "We shall easily manage him."

The Marquise looked at Rastignac, who bent over her. "That is the sort of man," murmured the dandy in her ear, "who is trusted to pass judgments on the life and interests of private individuals."

Like most men who have grown old in a business, Popinot readily let himself follow the habits he had acquired, more particularly habits of mind. His conversation was all of "the shop." He was fond of questioning those he talked to, forcing them to unexpected conclusions, making them tell more than they wished to reveal. Pozzo di Borgo, it is said, used to amuse himself by discovering other folks' secrets, and entangling them in his diplomatic snares, and thus, by invincible habit, showed how his mind was soaked in wiliness. As soon as Popinot had surveyed the ground, so to speak, on which he stood, he saw that it would be necessary to have recourse to the cleverest subtleties, the most elaborately wrapped up and disguised, which were in use in the Courts, to detect the truth.

Bianchon sat cold and stern, as a man who has made up his mind to endure torture without revealing his sufferings; but in his heart he wished that his uncle could only trample on this woman as we trample on a viper--a comparison suggested to him by the Marquise's long dress, by the curve of her attitude, her long neck, small head, and undulating movements.

"Well, monsieur," said Madame d'Espard, "however great my dislike to be or seem selfish, I have been suffering too long not to wish that you may settle matters at once. Shall I soon get a favorable decision?"

"Madame, I will do my best to bring matters to a conclusion," said Popinot, with an air of frank good-nature. "Are you ignorant of the reason which made the separation necessary which now subsists between you and the Marquis d'Espard?"

"Yes, monsieur," she replied, evidently prepared with a story to tell. "At the beginning of 1816 M. d'Espard, whose temper had completely changed within three months or so, proposed that we should go to live on one of his estates near Briancon, without any regard for my health, which that climate would have destroyed, or for my habits of life; I refused to go. My refusal gave rise to such unjustifiable reproaches on his part, that from that hour I had my suspicions as to the soundness of his mind. On the following day he left me, leaving me his house and the free use of my own income, and he went to live in the Rue de la Montagne-Sainte-Geneviève, taking with him my two children----"

"One moment, madame," said the lawyer, interrupting her. "What was that income?"

"Twenty-six thousand francs a year," she replied parenthetically. "I at once consulted old M. Bordin as to what I ought to do," she went on; "but it seems that there are so many difficulties in the way of depriving a father of the care of his children, that I was forced to resign myself to remaining alone at the age of twenty-two--an age at which many young women do very foolish things. You have read my petition, no doubt, monsieur; you know the principal facts on which I rely to procure a Commission in Lunacy with regard to M. d'Espard?"

"Have you ever applied to him, madame, to obtain the care of your children?"

"Yes, monsieur; but in vain. It is very hard on a mother to be deprived of the affection of her children, particularly when they can give her such happiness as every woman clings to."

"The elder must be sixteen," said Popinot.

"Fifteen," said the Marquise eagerly.

Here Bianchon and Rastignac looked at each other. Madame d'Espard bit her lips.

"What can the age of my children matter to you?"

"Well, madame," said the lawyer, without seeming to attach any importance to his words, "a lad of fifteen and his brother, of thirteen, I suppose, have legs and their wits about them; they might come to see you on the sly. If they do not, it is because they obey their father, and to obey him in that matter they must love him very dearly."

"I do not understand," said the Marquise.

"You do not know, perhaps," replied Popinot, "that in your petition your attorney represents your children as being very unhappy with their father?"

Madame d'Espard replied with charming innocence:

"I do not know what my attorney may have put into my mouth."

"Forgive my inferences," said Popinot, "but Justice weighs everything. What I ask you, madame, is suggested by my wish thoroughly to understand the matter. By your account M. d'Espard deserted you on the most frivolous pretext. Instead of going to Briancon, where he wished to take you, he remained in Paris. This point is not clear. Did he know this Madame Jeanrenaud before his marriage?"

"No, monsieur," replied the Marquise, with some asperity, visible only to Rastignac and the Chevalier d'Espard.

She was offended at being cross-examined by this layer when she had intended to beguile his judgment; but as Popinot still looked stupid from sheer absence of mind, she ended by attributing his interrogatory to the Questioning Spirit of Voltaire's bailiff.

"My parents," she went on, "married me at the age of sixteen to M. d'Espard, whose name, fortune, and mode of life were such as my family looked for in the man who was to be my husband. M. d'Espard was then six-and-twenty; he was a gentleman in the English sense of the word; his manners pleased me, he seemed to have plenty of ambition, and I like ambitious people," she added, looking at Rastignac. "If M. d'Espard had never met that Madame Jeanrenaud, his character, his learning, his acquirements would have raised him--as his friends then believed--to high office in the Government. King Charles X., at that time Monsieur, had the greatest esteem for him, and a peer's seat, an appointment at Court, some important post certainly would have been his. That woman turned his head, and has ruined all the prospects of my family."

"What were M. d'Espard's religious opinions at that time?"

"He was, and is still, a very pious man."

"You do not suppose that Madame Jeanrenaud may have influenced him by mysticism?"

"No, monsieur."

"You have a very fine house, madame," said Popinot suddenly, taking his hands out of his pockets, and rising to pick up his coat-tails and warm himself. "This boudoir is very nice, those chairs are magnificent, the whole apartment is sumptuous. You must indeed be most unhappy when, seeing yourself here, you know that your children are ill lodged, ill clothed, and ill fed. I can imagine nothing more terrible for a mother."

"Yes, indeed. I should be so glad to give the poor little fellows some amusement, while their father keeps them at work from morning till night at that wretched history of China."

"You give handsome balls; they would enjoy them, but they might acquire a taste for dissipation. However, their father might send them to you once or twice in the course of the winter."

"He brings them here on my birthday and on New Year's Day. On those days M. d'Espard does me the favor of dining here with them."

"It is very singular behaviour," said the judge, with an air of conviction. "Have you ever seen this Dame Jeanrenaud?"

"My brother-in-law one day, out of interest in his brother----"

"Ah! monsieur is M. d'Espard's brother?" said the lawyer, interrupting her.

The Chevalier bowed, but did not speak.

"M. d'Espard, who has watched this affair, took me to the Oratoire, where this woman goes to sermon, for she is a Protestant. I saw her; she is not in the least attractive; she looks like a butcher's wife, extremely fat, horribly marked with the smallpox; she has feet and hands like a man's, she squints, in short, she is monstrous!"

"It is inconceivable," said the judge, looking like the most imbecile judge in the whole kingdom. "And this creature lives near here, Rue Verte, in a fine house? There are no plain folk left, it would seem?"

"In a mansion on which her son has spent absurd sums."

"Madame," said Popinot, "I live in the Faubourg Saint-Marceau; I know nothing of such expenses. What do you call absurd sums?"

"Well," said the Marquise, "a stable with five horses and three carriages, a phaeton, a brougham, and a cabriolet."

"That costs a large sum, then?" asked Popinot in surprise.

"Enormous sums!" said Rastignac, intervening. "Such an establishment would cost, for the stables, the keeping the carriages in order, and the liveries for the men, between fifteen and sixteen thousand francs a year."

"Should you think so, madame?" said the judge, looking much astonished.

"Yes, at least," replied the Marquise.

"And the furniture, too, must have cost a lot of money?"

"More than a hundred thousand francs," replied Madame d'Espard, who could not help smiling at the lawyer's vulgarity.

"Judges, madame, are apt to be incredulous; it is what they are paid for, and

I am incredulous. The Baron Jeanrenaud and his mother must have fleeced M. d'Espard most preposterously, if what you say is correct. There is a stable establishment which, by your account, costs sixteen thousand francs a year. Housekeeping, servants' wages, and the gross expenses of the house itself must run to twice as much; that makes a total of from fifty to sixty thousand francs a year. Do you suppose that these people, formerly so extremely poor, can have so large a fortune? A million yields scarcely forty thousand a year."

"Monsieur, the mother and son invested the money given them by M. d'Espard in the funds when they were at 60 to 80. I should think their income must be more than sixty thousand francs. And then the son has fine appointments."

"If they spend sixty thousand francs a year," said the judge, "how much do you spend?"

"Well," said Madame d'Espard, "about the same." The Chevalier started a little, the Marquise colored; Bianchon looked at Rastignac; but Popinot preserved an expression of simplicity which quite deceived Madame d'Espard. The chevalier took no part in the conversation; he saw that all was lost.

"These people, madame, might be indicted before the superior Court," said Popinot.

"That was my opinion," exclaimed the Marquise, enchanted. "If threatened with the police, they would have come to terms."

"Madame," said Popinot, "when M. d'Espard left you, did he not give you a power of attorney enabling you to manage and control your own affairs?"

"I do not understand the object of all these questions," said the Marquise with petulance. "It seems to me that if you would only consider the state in which I am placed by my husband's insanity, you ought to be troubling yourself about him, and not about me."

"We are coming to that, madame," said the judge. "Before placing in your hands, or in any others, the control of M. d'Espard's property, supposing he were pronounced incapable, the Court must inquire as to how you have managed your own. If M. d'Espard gave you the power, he would have shown confidence in you, and the Court would recognize the fact. Had you any power from him? You might have bought or sold house property or invested money in business?"

"No, monsieur, the Blamont-Chauvrys are not in the habit of trading," said she, extremely nettled in her pride as an aristocrat, and forgetting the business in hand. "My property is intact, and M. d'Espard gave me no power to act."

The Chevalier put his hand over his eyes not to betray the vexation he felt at his sister-in-law's short-sightedness, for she was ruining herself by her answers. Popinot had gone straight to the mark in spite of his apparent doublings.

"Madame," said the lawyer, indicating the Chevalier, "this gentleman, of course, is your near connection? May we speak openly before these other gentlemen?"

"Speak on," said the Marquise, surprised at this caution.

"Well, madame, granting that you spend only sixty thousand francs a year, to any one who sees your stables, your house, your train of servants, and a style of housekeeping which strikes me as far more luxurious than that of the Jeanrenauds, that sum would seem well laid out."

The Marquise bowed an agreement.

"But," continued the judge, "if you have no more than twenty-six thousand francs a year, you may have a hundred thousand francs of debt. The Court would therefore have a right to imagine that the motives which prompt you to ask that your husband may be deprived of the control of his property are complicated by self-interest and the need of paying your debts--if--you--have--any. The requests addressed to me have interested me in your position; consider fully and make your confession. If my suppositions have hit the truth, there is yet time to avoid the blame which the Court would have a perfect right to express in the saving clauses of the verdict if you could not show your attitude to be absolutely honorable and clear.

"It is our duty to examine the motives of the applicant as well as to listen to the plea of the witness under examination, to ascertain whether the petitioner may not have been prompted by passion, by a desire for money, which is unfortunately too common----"

The Marquise was on Saint Laurence's gridiron.

"And I must have explanations on this point. Madame, I have no wish to call you to account; I only want to know how you have managed to live at the rate of sixty thousand francs a year, and that for some years past. There are plenty of women who achieve this in their housekeeping, but you are not one of those. Tell me, you may have the most legitimate resources, a royal pension, or some claim on the indemnities lately granted; but even then you must have had your husband's authority to receive them."

The Marquise did not speak.

"You must remember," Popinot went on, "that M. d'Espard may wish to enter a protest, and his counsel will have a right to find out whether you have any creditors. This boudoir is newly furnished, your rooms are not now furnished with the things left to you by M. d'Espard in 1816. If, as you did me the honor of informing me, furniture is costly for the Jeanrenauds, it must be yet more so for you, who are a great lady. Though I am a judge, I am but a man; I may be wrong--tell me so. Remember the duties imposed on me by the law, and the rigorous inquiries it demands, when the case before it is the suspension from all his functions of the father of a family in the prime of life. So you will pardon me, Madame la Marquise, for laying all these difficulties before you; it will be easy for you to give me an explanation.

"When a man is pronounced incapable of the control of his own affairs, a trustee has to be appointed. Who will be the trustee?"

"His brother," said the Marquise.

The Chevalier bowed. There was a short silence, very uncomfortable for the five persons who were present. The judge, in sport as it were, had laid open the woman's sore place. Popinot's countenance of common, clumsy good-nature, at which the Marquise, the Chevalier, and Rastignac had been inclined to laugh, had gained importance in their eyes. As they stole a look at him, they discerned the various expressions of that eloquent mouth. The ridiculous mortal was a judge of acumen. His studious notice of the boudoir was accounted for: he had started from the gilt elephant supporting the chimney-clock, examining all this luxury, and had ended by reading this woman's soul.

"If the Marquis d'Espard is mad about China, I see that you are not less fond of its products," said Popinot, looking at the porcelain on the chimney-piece. "But perhaps it was from M. le Marquis that you had these charming Oriental pieces," and he pointed to some precious trifles.

This irony, in very good taste, made Bianchon smile, and petrified Rastignac, while the Marquise bit her thin lips.

"Instead of being the protector of a woman placed in a cruel dilemma --an alternative between losing her fortune and her children, and being regarded as her husband's enemy," she said, "you accuse me, monsieur! You suspect my motives! You must own that your conduct is strange!"

"Madame," said the judge eagerly, "the caution exercised by the Court in such cases as these might have given you, in any other judge, a perhaps less indulgent critic than I am.--And do you suppose that M. d'Espard's lawyer will show you any great consideration? Will he not be suspicious of motives which may be perfectly pure and disinterested? Your life will be at his mercy; he will inquire into it without qualifying his search by the respectful deference I have for you."

"I am much obliged to you, monsieur," said the Marquise satirically. "Admitting for the moment that I owe thirty thousand or fifty thousand francs, in the first place, it would be a mere trifle to the d'Espards and the Blamont-Chauvrys. But if my husband is not in the possession of his mental faculties, would that prevent his being pronounced incapable?"

"No, madame," said Popinot.

"Although you have questioned me with a sort of cunning which I should not have suspected in a judge, and under circumstances where straightforwardness would have answered your purpose," she went on, "I will tell you without subterfuge that my position in the world, and the efforts I have to make to keep up my connection, are not in the least to my taste. I began my life by a long period of solitude; but my children's interest appealed to me; I felt that I must fill their father's place. By receiving my friends, by keeping up all this connection, by contracting these debts, I have secured their future welfare; I have prepared for them a brilliant career where they will find help and favor; and to have what has thus been acquired, many a man of business, lawyer or banker, would gladly pay all it has cost me."

"I appreciate your devoted conduct, madame," replied Popinot. "It does you honor, and I blame you for nothing. A judge belongs to all: he must know and weigh every fact."

Madame d'Espard's tact and practice in estimating men made her understand that M. Popinot was not to be influenced by any consideration. She had counted on an ambitious lawyer, she had found a man of conscience. She at once thought of finding other means for securing the success of her side.

The servants brought in tea.

"Have you any further explanations to give me, madame?" said Popinot, seeing these preparations.

"Monsieur," she replied haughtily, "do your business your own way; question M. d'Espard, and you will pity me, I am sure." She raised her head, looking Popinot in the face with pride, mingled with impertinence; the worthy man bowed himself out respectfully.

"A nice man is your uncle," said Rastignac to Bianchon. "Is he really so dense? Does not he know what the Marquise d'Espard is, what her influence means, her unavowed power over people? The Keeper of the Seals will be with her to-morrow ---"

"My dear fellow, how can I help it?" said Bianchon. "Did not I warn you? He is not a man you can get over."

"No," said Rastignac; "he is a man you must run over."

The doctor was obliged to make his bow to the Marquise and her mute Chevalier to catch up Popinot, who, not being the man to endure an embarrassing position, was pacing through the rooms.

"That woman owes a hundred thousand crowns," said the judge, as he stepped into his nephew's cab.

"And what do you think of the case?"

"I," said the judge. "I never have an opinion till I have gone into everything. To-morrow early I will send to Madame Jeanrenaud to call on me in my private office at four o'clock, to make her explain the facts which concern her, for she is compromised."

"I should very much like to know what the end will be."

"Why, bless me, do not you see that the Marquise is the tool of that tall lean man who never uttered a word? There is a strain of Cain in him, but of the Cain who goes to the Law Courts for his bludgeon, and there, unluckily for him, we keep more than one Damocles' sword."

"Oh, Rastignac! what brought you into that boat, I wonder?" exclaimed Bianchon.

"Ah, we are used to seeing these little family conspiracies," said Popinot. "Not a year passes without a number of verdicts of 'insufficient evidence' against applications of this kind. In our state of society such an attempt brings no dishonor, while we send a poor devil to the galleys who breaks a pane of glass dividing him from a bowl full of gold. Our Code is not faultless."

"But these are the facts?"

"My boy, do you not know all the judicial romances with which clients impose on their attorneys? If the attorneys condemned themselves to state nothing but the truth, they would not earn enough to keep their office open."

Next day, at four in the afternoon, a very stout dame, looking a good deal like a cask dressed up in a gown and belt, mounted Judge Popinot's stairs, perspiring and panting. She had, with great difficulty, got out of a green landau, which suited her to a miracle; you could not think of the woman without the landau, or the landau without the woman.

"It is I, my dear sir," said she, appearing in the doorway of the judge's room. "Madame Jeanrenaud, whom you summoned exactly as if I were a thief, neither more nor less."

The common words were spoken in a common voice, broken by the wheezing of asthma, and ending in a cough.

"When I go through a damp place, I can't tell you what I suffer, sir. I shall never make old bones, saving your presence. However, here I am."

The lawyer was quite amazed at the appearance of this supposed Marechale d'Ancre. Madame Jeanrenaud's face was pitted with an infinite number of little holes, was very red, with a pug nose and a low forehead, and was as round as a ball; for everything about the good woman was round. She had the bright eyes of a country woman, an honest gaze, a cheerful tone, and chestnut hair held in place by a bonnet cap under a green bonnet decked with a shabby bunch of auriculas. Her stupendous bust was a thing to laugh at, for it made one fear some grotesque explosion every time she coughed. Her enormous legs were of the shape which make the Paris street boy describe such a woman as being built on piles. The widow wore a green gown trimmed with chinchilla, which looked on her as a splash of dirty oil would look on a bride's veil. In short, everything about her harmonized with her last words: "Here I am."

"Madame," said Popinot, "you are suspected of having used some seductive arts to induce M. d'Espard to hand over to you very considerable sums of money."

"Of what! of what!" cried she. "Of seductive arts? But, my dear sir, you are a man to be respected, and, moreover, as a lawyer you ought to have some good sense. Look at me! Tell me if I am likely to seduce any one. I cannot tie my own shoes, nor even stoop. For these twenty years past, the Lord be praised, I have not dared to put on a pair of stays under pain of sudden death. I was as thin as an asparagus stalk when I was seventeen, and pretty too--I may say so now. So I married Jeanrenaud, a good fellow, and headman on the salt-barges. I had my boy, who is a fine young man; he is my pride, and it is not holding myself cheap to say he is my best piece of work. My little Jeanrenaud was a soldier who did Napoleon credit, and who served in the Imperial Guard. But, alas! at the death of my old man, who was drowned, times changed for the worse. I had the smallpox. I was kept two years in my room without stirring, and I came out of it the size you see me, hideous for ever, and as wretched as could be. These are my seductive arts."

"But what, then, can the reasons be that have induced M. d'Espard to give you sums----"

"Hugious sums, monsieur, say the word; I do not mind. But as to his reasons, I am not at liberty to explain them."

"You are wrong. At this moment, his family, very naturally alarmed, are about to bring an action----"

"Heavens above us!" said the good woman, starting up. "Is it possible that he should be worried on my account? That king of men, a man that has not his match! Rather than he should have the smallest trouble, or hair less on his head I could almost say, we would return every sou, monsieur. Write that down on your papers. Heaven above us! I will go at once and tell Jeanrenaud what is going on! A pretty thing indeed!"

And the little old woman went out, rolled herself downstairs, and disappeared.

"That one tells no lies," said Popinot to himself. "Well, to-morrow I shall know the whole story, for I shall go to see the Marquis d'Espard."

People who have outlived the age when a man wastes his vitality at random, know how great an influence may be exercised on more important events by apparently trivial incidents, and will not be surprised at the weight here given to the following minor fact. Next day Popinot had an attack of coryza, a complaint which is not dangerous, and generally known by the absurd and inadequate name of a cold in the head.

The judge, who could not suppose that the delay could be serious, feeling himself a little feverish, kept his room, and did not go to see the Marquis d'Espard. This day lost was, to this affair, what on the Day of Dupes the cup of soup had been, taken by Marie de Medici, which, by delaying her meeting with Louis XIII., enabled Richelieu to arrive at Saint-Germain before her, and recapture his royal slave.

Before accompanying the lawyer and his registering clerk to the Marquis d'Espard's house, it may be as well to glance at the home and the private affairs of this father of sons whom his wife's petition represented to be a madman.

Here and there in the old parts of Paris a few buildings may still be seen in which the archaeologist can discern an intention of decorating the city, and that love of property, which leads the owner to give a durable character to the structure. The house in which M. d'Espard was then living, in the Rue de la Montagne-Sainte-Genevieve, was one of these old mansions, built in stone, and not devoid of a certain richness of style; but time had blackened the stone, and revolutions in the town had damaged it both outside and inside. The dignitaries who formerly dwelt in the neighborhood of the University having disappeared with the great ecclesiastical foundations, this house had become the home of industries and of inhabitants whom it was never destined to shelter. During the last century a printing establishment had worn down the polished floors, soiled the carved wood, blackened the walls, and altered the principal internal arrangements. Formerly the residence of a Cardinal, this fine house was now divided among plebeian tenants. The character of the architecture showed that it had been built under the reigns of Henry III., Henry IV., and Louis XIII., at the time when the hotels Mignon and Serpente were erected in the same neighborhood, with the palace of the Princess Palatine, and the Sorbonne. An old man could remember having heard it called, in the last century, the hotel Duperron, so it seemed probable that the illustrious Cardinal of that name had built, or perhaps merely lived in it.

There still exists, indeed, in the corner of the courtyard, a perron or flight of several outer steps by which the house is entered; and the way into the garden on the garden front is down a similar flight of steps. In spite of dilapidations, the luxury lavished by the architect on the balustrade and entrance porch crowning these two perrons suggests the simple-minded purpose of commemorating the owner's name, a sort of sculptured pun which our ancestors often allowed themselves. Finally, in support of this evidence, archaeologists can still discern in the medallions which show on the principal front some traces of the cords of the Roman hat.

M. le Marquis d'Espard lived on the ground floor, in order, no doubt, to enjoy the garden, which might be called spacious for that neighborhood, and which lay open for his children's health. The situation of the house, in a street on a steep hill, as its name indicates, secured these ground-floor rooms against ever being damp. M. d'Espard had taken them, no doubt, for a very moderate price, rents being low at the time when he settled in that quarter, in order to be among the schools and to superintend his boys' education. Moreover, the state in which he found the place, with everything to repair, had no doubt induced the owner to be accommodating. Thus M. d'Espard had been able to go to some expense to settle himself suitably without being accused of extravagance. The loftiness of the rooms, the paneling, of which nothing survived but the frames, the decoration of the ceilings, all displayed the dignity which the prelacy stamped on whatever it attempted or created, and which artists discern to this day in the smallest relic that remains, though it be but a book, a dress, the panel of a bookcase, or an armchair.

The Marquis had the rooms painted in the rich brown tones loved of the Dutch and of the citizens of Old Paris, hues which lend such good effects to the painter of genre. The panels were hung with plain paper in harmony with the paint. The window curtains were of inexpensive materials, but chosen so as to produce a generally happy result; the furniture was not too crowded and judiciously placed. Any one on going into this home could not resist a sense of sweet peacefulness, produced by the perfect calm, the stillness which prevailed, by the unpretentious unity of color, the keeping of the picture, in the words a painter might use. A certain nobleness in the details, the exquisite cleanliness of the furniture, and a perfect concord of men and things, all brought the word "suavity" to the lips.

Few persons were admitted to the rooms used by the Marquis and his two sons, whose life might perhaps seem mysterious to their neighbors. In a wing towards the street, on the third floor, there are three large rooms which had been left in the state of dilapidation and grotesque bareness to which they had been reduced by the printing works. These three rooms, devoted to the evolution of the Picturesque History of China, were contrived to serve as a writing-room, a depository, and a private room, where M. d'Espard sat during part of the day; for after breakfast till four in the afternoon the Marquis remained in this room on the third floor to work at the publication he had undertaken. Visitors wanting to see him commonly found him there, and often the two boys on their return from school resorted thither. Thus the ground-floor rooms were a sort of sanctuary where the father and sons spent their time from the hour of dinner till the next day, and his domestic life was carefully closed against the public eye.

His only servants were a cook--an old woman who had long been attached to his family--and a man-servant forty years old, who was with him when he married Mademoiselle de Blamont. His children's nurse had also remained with them, and the minute care to which the apartment bore witness revealed the sense of order and the maternal affections expended by this woman in her master's interest, in the management of his house, and the charge of his children. These three good souls, grave, and uncommunicative folk, seemed to have entered into the idea which ruled the Marquis' domestic life. And the contrast between their habits and those of most servants was a peculiarity which cast an air of mystery over the house, and fomented the calumny to which M. d'Espard himself lent occasion. Very laudable motives had made him determine never to be on visiting terms with any of the other tenants in the house. In undertaking to educate his boys he wished to keep them from all contact with strangers. Perhaps, too, he wished to avoid the intrusion of neighbors.

In a man of his rank, at a time when the Quartier Latin was distracted by Liberalism, such conduct was sure to rouse in opposition a host of petty passions, of feelings whose folly is only to be measured by their meanness, the outcome of porters' gossip and malevolent tattle from door to door, all unknown to M. d'Espard and his retainers. His man-servant was stigmatized as a Jesuit, his cook as a sly fox; the nurse was in collusion with Madame Jeanrenaud to rob the madman. The madman was the Marquis. By degrees the other tenants came to regard as proofs of madness a number of things they had noticed in M. d'Espard, and passed through the sieve of their judgment without discerning any reasonable motive for them.

Having no belief in the success of the History of China, they had managed to convince the landlord of the house that M. d'Espard had no money just at a time when, with the forgetfulness which often befalls busy men, he had allowed the tax-collector to send him a summons for non-payment of arrears. The landlord forthwith claimed his quarter's rent from January 1st by sending in a receipt, which the porter's wife had amused herself by detaining. On the 15th a summons to pay was served on M. d'Espard, the portress had delivered it at her leisure, and he supposed it to be some misunderstanding, not conceiving of any incivility from a man in whose house he had been living for twelve years. The Marquis was actually seized by a bailiff at the time when his man-servant had gone to carry the money for the rent to the landlord.

This arrest, assiduously reported to the persons with whom he was in treaty for his undertaking, had alarmed some of them who were already doubtful of M. d'Espard's solvency in consequence of the enormous sums which Baron Jeanrenaud and his mother were said to be receiving from him. And, indeed, these suspicions on the part of the tenants, the creditors, and the landlord had some excuse in the Marquis' extreme economy in housekeeping. He conducted it as a ruined man might. His servants always paid in ready money for the most trifling necessaries of life, and acted as not choosing to take credit; if now they had asked for anything on credit, it would probably have been refused, calumnious gossip had been so widely believed in the neighborhood. There are tradesmen who like those of their customers who pay badly when they see them often, while they hate others, and very good ones, who hold themselves on too high a level to allow of any familiarity as CHUMS, a vulgar but expressive word. Men are made so; in almost every class they will allow to a gossip, or a vulgar soul that flatters them, facilities and favors they refuse to the superiority they resent, in whatever form it may show itself. The shopkeeper who rails at the Court has his courtiers.

In short, the manners of the Marquis and his children were certain to arouse ill-feeling in their neighbors, and to work them up by degrees to the pitch of malevolence when men do not hesitate at an act of meanness if only it may damage the adversary they have themselves created.

M. d'Espard was a gentleman, as his wife was a lady, by birth and breeding; noble types, already so rare in France that the observer can easily count the persons who perfectly realize them. These two characters are based on primitive ideas, on beliefs that may be called innate, on habits formed in infancy, and which have ceased to exist. To believe in pure blood, in a privileged race, to stand in thought above other men, must we not from birth have measured the distance which divides patricians from the mob? To command, must we not have never met our equal? And finally, must not education inculcate the ideas with which Nature inspires those great men on whose brow she has placed a crown before their mother has ever set a kiss there? These ideas, this education, are no longer possible in France, where for forty years past chance has arrogated the right of making noblemen by dipping them in the blood of battles, by gilding them with glory, by crowning them with the halo of genius; where the abolition of entail and of eldest sonship, by frittering away estates, compels the nobleman to attend to his own business instead of attending to affairs of state, and where personal greatness can only be such greatness as is acquired by long and patient toil: quite a new era.

Regarded as a relic of that great institution know as feudalism, M. d'Espard deserved respectful admiration. If he believed himself to be by blood the superior of other men, he also believed in all the obligations of nobility; he had the virtues and the strength it demands. He had brought up his children in his own principles, and taught them from the cradle the religion of their caste. A deep sense of their own dignity, pride of name, the conviction that they were by birth great, gave rise in them to a kingly pride, the courage of knights, and the protecting kindness of a baronial lord; their manners, harmonizing with their notions, would have become princes, and offended all the world of the Rue de la Montagne-Sainte-Genevieve --a world, above all others, of equality, where every one believed that M. d'Espard was ruined, and where all, from the lowest to the highest, refused the privileges of nobility to a nobleman without money, because they were all ready to allow an enriched bourgeois to usurp them. Thus the lack of communion between this family and other persons was as much moral as it was physical.

In the father and the children alike, their personality harmonized with the spirit within. M. d'Espard, at this time about fifty, might have sat as a model to represent the aristocracy of birth in the nineteenth century. He was slight and fair; there was in the outline and general expression of his face a native distinction which spoke of lofty sentiments, but it bore the impress of a deliberate coldness which commanded respect a little too decidedly. His aquiline nose bent at the tip from left to right, a slight crookedness which was not devoid of grace; his blue eyes, his high forehead, prominent enough at the brows to form a thick ridge that checked the light and shaded his eyes, all indicated a spirit of rectitude, capable of perseverance and perfect loyalty, while it gave a singular look to his countenance. This penthouse forehead might, in fact, hint at a touch of madness, and his thick-knitted eyebrows added to the apparent eccentricity. He had the white well-kept hands of a gentleman; his foot was high and narrow. His hesitating speech--not merely as to his pronunciation, which was that of a stammerer, but also in the expression of his ideas, his thought and language--produced on the mind of the hearer the impression of a man who, in familiar phraseology, comes and goes, feels his way, tries everything, breaks off his gestures, and finishes nothing. This defect was purely superficial, and in contrast with the decisiveness of a firmly-set mouth, and the strongly-marked character of his physiognomy. His rather jerky gait matched his mode of speech. These peculiarities helped to affirm his supposed insanity. In spite of his elegant appearance, he was systematically parsimonious in his personal expenses, and wore the same black frock-coat for three or four years, brushed with extreme care by his old man-servant.

As to the children, they both were handsome, and endowed with a grace which did not exclude an expression of aristocratic disdain. They had the bright coloring, the clear eye, the transparent flesh which reveal habits of purity, regularity of life, and a due proportion of work and play. They both had black hair and blue eyes, and a twist in their nose, like their father; but their mother, perhaps, had transmitted to them the dignity of speech, of look and mien, which are hereditary in the Blamont-Chauvrys. Their voices, as clear as crystal, had an emotional quality, the softness which proves so seductive; they had, in short, the voice a woman would willingly listen to after feeling the flame of their looks. But, above all, they had the modesty of pride, a chaste reserve, a /touch-me-not/ which at a maturer age might have seemed intentional coyness, so much did their demeanor inspire a wish to know them. The elder, Comte Clement de Negrepelisse, was close upon his sixteenth year. For the last two years he had ceased to wear the pretty English round jacket which his brother, Vicomte Camille d'Espard, still wore. The Count, who for the last six months went no more to the College Henri IV., was dressed in the style of a young man enjoying the first pleasures of fashion. His father had not wished to condemn him to a year's useless study of philosophy; he was trying to give his knowledge some consistency by the study of transcendental mathematics. At the same time, the Marquis was having him taught Eastern languages, the international law of Europe, heraldry, and history from the original sources, charters, early documents, and collections of edicts. Camille had lately begun to study rhetoric.

The day when Popinot arranged to go to question M. d'Espard was a Thursday, a holiday. At about nine in the morning, before their father was awake, the brothers were playing in the garden. Clement was finding it hard to refuse his brother, who was anxious to go to the shooting-gallery for the first time, and who begged him to second his request to the Marquis. The Viscount always rather took advantage of his weakness, and was very fond of wrestling with his brother. So the couple were quarreling and fighting in play like schoolboys. As they ran in the garden, chasing each other, they made so much noise as to wake their father, who came to the window without their perceiving him in the heat of the fray. The Marquis amused himself with watching his two children twisted together like snakes, their faces flushed by the exertion of their strength; their complexion was rose and white, their eyes flashed sparks, their limbs writhed like cords in the fire; they fell, sprang up again, and caught each other like athletes in a circus, affording their father one of those moments of happiness which would make amends for the keenest anxieties of a busy life. Two other persons, one on the second and one on the first floor, were also looking into the garden, and saying that the old madman was amusing himself by making his children fight. Immediately a number of heads appeared at the windows; the Marquis, noticing them, called a word to his sons, who at once climbed up to the window and jumped into his room, and Clement obtained the permission asked by Camille.

All through the house every one was talking of the Marquis' new form of insanity. When Popinot arrived at about twelve o'clock, accompanied by his clerk, the portress, when asked for M. d'Espard, conducted him to the third floor, telling him "as how M. d'Espard, no longer ago than that very morning, had set on his two children to fight, and laughed like the monster he was on seeing the younger biting the elder till he bled, and as how no doubt he longed to see them kill each other.-- Don't ask me the reason why," she added; "he doesn't show himself!"

Just as the woman spoke these decisive words, she had brought the judge to the landing on the third floor, face to face with a door covered with notices announcing the successive numbers of the Picturesque History of China. The muddy floor, the dirty banisters, the door where the printers had left their marks, the dilapidated window, and the ceiling on which the apprentices had amused themselves with drawing monstrosities with the smoky flare of their tallow dips, the piles of paper and litter heaped up in the corners, intentionally or from sheer neglect--in short, every detail of the picture lying before his eyes, agreed so well with the facts alleged by the Marquise that the judge, in spite of his impartiality, could not help believing them.

"There you are, gentlemen," said the porter's wife; "there is the manifactor, where the Chinese swallow up enough to feed the whole neighborhood."

The clerk looked at the judge with a smile, and Popinot found it hard to keep his countenance. They went together into the outer room, where sat an old man, who, no doubt, performed the functions of office clerk, shopman, and cashier. This old man was the Maitre Jacques of China. Along the walls ran long shelves, on which the published numbers lay in piles. A partition in wood, with a grating lined with green curtains, cut off the end of the room, forming a private office. A till with a slit to admit or disgorge crown pieces indicated the cash-desk.

"M. d'Espard?" said Popinot, addressing the man, who wore a gray blouse.

The shopman opened the door into the next room, where the lawyer and his companion saw a venerable old man, white-headed and simply dressed, wearing the Cross of Saint-Louis, seated at a desk. He ceased comparing some sheets of colored prints to look up at the two visitors. This room was an unpretentious office, full of books and proof-sheets. There was a black wood table at which some one, at the moment absent, no doubt was accustomed to work.

"The Marquis d'Espard?" said Popinot.

"No, monsieur," said the old man, rising; "what do you want with him?" he added, coming forward, and showing by his demeanor the dignified manners and habits due to a gentlemanly education.

"We wish to speak with him on business exclusively personal to himself," replied Popinot.

"D'Espard, here are some gentlemen who want to see you," then said the old man, going into the furthest room, where the Marquis was sitting by the fire reading the newspaper.

This innermost room had a shabby carpet, the windows were hung with gray holland curtains; the furniture consisted of a few mahogany chairs, two armchairs, a desk with a revolving front, an ordinary office table, and on the chimney-shelf, a dingy clock and two old candlesticks. The old man led the way for Popinot and his registrar, and pulled forward two chairs, as though he were master of the place; M. d'Espard left it to him. After the preliminary civilities, during which the judge watched the supposed lunatic, the Marquis naturally asked what was the object of this visit. On this Popinot glanced significantly at the old gentleman and the Marquis.

"I believe, Monsieur le Marquis," said he, "that the character of my functions, and the inquiry that has brought me here, make it desirable that we should be alone, though it is understood by law that in such cases the inquiries have a sort of family publicity. I am judge on the Inferior Court of Appeal for the Department of the Seine, and charged by the President with the duty of examining you as to certain facts set forth in a petition for a Commission in Lunacy on the part of the Marquise d'Espard."

The old man withdrew. When the lawyer and the Marquis were alone, the clerk shut the door, and seated himself unceremoniously at the office table, where he laid out his papers and prepared to take down his notes. Popinot had still kept his eye on M. d'Espard; he was watching the effect on him of this crude statement, so painful for a man in full possession of his reason. The Marquis d'Espard, whose face was usually pale, as are those of fair men, suddenly turned scarlet with anger; he trembled for an instant, sat down, laid his paper on the chimney-piece, and looked down. In a moment he had recovered his gentlemanly dignity, and looked steadily at the judge, as if to read in his countenance the indications of his character.

"How is it, monsieur," he asked, "that I have had no notice of such a petition?"

"Monsieur le Marquis, persons on whom such a commission is held not being supposed to have the use of their reason, any notice of the petition is unnecessary. The duty of the Court chiefly consists in verifying the allegations of the petitioner."

"Nothing can be fairer," replied the Marquis. "Well, then, monsieur, be so good as to tell me what I ought to do----"

"You have only to answer my questions, omitting nothing. However delicate the reasons may be which may have led you to act in such a manner as to give Madame d'Espard a pretext for her petition, speak without fear. It is unnecessary to assure you that lawyers know their duties, and that in such cases the profoundest secrecy----"

"Monsieur," said the Marquis, whose face expressed the sincerest pain, "if my explanations should lead to any blame being attached to Madame d'Espard's conduct, what will be the result?"

"The Court may add its censure to its reasons for its decision."

"Is such censure optional? If I were to stipulate with you, before replying, that nothing should be said that could annoy Madame d'Espard in the event of your report being in my favor, would the Court take my request into consideration?"

The judge looked at the Marquis, and the two men exchanged sentiments of equal magnanimity.

"Noel," said Popinot to his registrar, "go into the other room. If you can be of use, I will call you in.--If, as I am inclined to think," he went on, speaking to the Marquis when the clerk had gone out, "I find that there is some misunderstanding in this case, I can promise you, monsieur, that on your application the Court will act with due courtesy.

"There is a leading fact put forward by Madame d'Espard, the most serious of all, of which I must beg for an explanation," said the judge after a pause. "It refers to the dissipation of your fortune to the advantage of a certain Madame Jeanrenaud, the widow of a bargemaster--or rather, to that of her son, Colonel Jeanrenaud, for whom you are said to have procured an appointment, to have exhausted your influence with the King, and at last to have extended such protection as secures him a good marriage. The petition suggests that such a friendship is more devoted than any feelings, even those which morality must disapprove----"

A sudden flush crimsoned the Marquis' face and forehead, tears even started to his eyes, for his eyelashes were wet, then wholesome pride crushed the emotions, which in a man are accounted a weakness.

"To tell you the truth, monsieur," said the Marquis, in a broken voice, "you place me in a strange dilemma. The motives of my conduct were to have died with me. To reveal them I must disclose to you some secret wounds, must place the honor of my family in your keeping, and must speak of myself, a delicate matter, as you will fully understand. I hope, monsieur, that it will all remain a secret between us. You will, no doubt, be able to find in the formulas of the law one which will allow of judgment being pronounced without any betrayal of my confidences."

"So far as that goes, it is perfectly possible, Monsieur le Marquis."

"Some time after my marriage," said M. d'Espard, "my wife having run into considerable expenses, I was obliged to have recourse to borrowing. You know what was the position of noble families during the Revolution; I had not been able to keep a steward or a man of business. Nowadays gentlemen are for the most part obliged to manage their affairs themselves. Most of my title-deeds had been brought to Paris, from Languedoc, Provence, or le Comtat, by my father, who dreaded, and not without reason, the inquisition which family title-deeds, and what was then styled the 'parchments' of the privileged class, brought down on the owners.

"Our name is Negrepelisse; d'Espard is a title acquired in the time of Henri IV. by a marriage which brought us the estates and titles of the house of d'Espard, on condition of our bearing an escutcheon of pretence on our coat-of-arms, those of the house of d'Espard, an old family of Bearn, connected in the female line with that of Albret: quarterly, paly of or and sable; and azure two griffins' claws armed, gules in saltire, with the famous motto Des partem leonis. At the time of this alliance we lost Negrepelisse, a little town which was as famous during the religious struggles as was my ancestor who then bore the name. Captain de Negrepelisse was ruined by the burning of all his property, for the Protestants did not spare a friend of Montluc's.

"The Crown was unjust to M. de Negrepelisse; he received neither a marshal's baton, nor a post as governor, nor any indemnity; King Charles IX., who was fond of him, died without being able to reward him; Henri IV. arranged his marriage with Mademoiselle d'Espard, and secured him the estates of that house, but all those of the Negrepelisses had already passed into the hands of his creditors.

"My great-grandfather, the Marquis d'Espard, was, like me, placed early in life at the head of his family by the death of his father, who, after dissipating his wife's fortune, left his son nothing but the entailed estates of the d'Espards, burdened with a jointure. The young Marquis was all the more straitened for money because he held a post at Court. Being in great favor with Louis XIV., the King's goodwill brought him a fortune. But here, monsieur, a blot stained our escutcheon, an unconfessed and horrible stain of blood and disgrace which I am making it my business to wipe out. I discovered the secret among the deeds relating to the estate of Negrepelisse and the packets of letters."

At this solemn moment the Marquis spoke without hesitation or any of the repetition habitual with him; but it is a matter of common observation that persons who, in ordinary life, are afflicted with these two defects, are freed from them as soon as any passionate emotion underlies their speech.

"The Revocation of the Edict of Nantes was decreed," he went on. "You are no doubt aware, monsieur, that this was an opportunity for many favorites to make their fortunes. Louis XIV. bestowed on the magnates about his Court the confiscated lands of those Protestant families who did not take the prescribed steps for the sale of their property. Some persons in high favor went 'Protestant-hunting,' as the phrase was. I have ascertained beyond a doubt that the fortune enjoyed to this day by two ducal families is derived from lands seized from hapless merchants.

"I will not attempt to explain to you, a man of law, all the manoeuvres employed to entrap the refugees who had large fortunes to carry away. It is enough to say that the lands of Negrepelisse, comprising twenty-two churches and rights over the town, and those of Gravenges which had formerly belonged to us, were at that time in the hands of a Protestant family. My grandfather recovered them by gift from Louis XIV. This gift was effected by documents hall-marked by atrocious iniquity. The owner of these two estates, thinking he would be able to return, had gone through the form of a sale, and was going to Switzerland to join his family, whom he had sent in advance. He wished, no doubt, to take advantage of every delay granted by the law, so as to settle the concerns of his business.

"This man was arrested by order of the governor, the trustee confessed the truth, the poor merchant was hanged, and my ancestor had the two estates. I would gladly have been able to ignore the share he took in the plot; but the governor was his uncle on the mother's side, and I have unfortunately read the letter in which he begged him to apply to Deodatus, the name agreed upon by the Court to designate the King. In this letter there is a tone of jocosity with reference to the victim, which filled me with horror. In the end, the sums of money sent by the refugee family to ransom the poor man were kept by the governor, who despatched the merchant all the same."

The Marquis paused, as though the memory of it were still too heavy for him to bear.

"This unfortunate family were named Jeanrenaud," he went on. "That name is enough to account for my conduct. I could never think without keen pain of the secret disgrace that weighed on my family. That fortune enabled my grandfather to marry a demoiselle de Navarreins-Lansac, heiress to the younger branch of that house, who were at that time much richer than the elder branch of the Navarreins. My father thus became one of the largest landowners in the kingdom. He was able to marry my mother, a Grandlieu of the younger branch. Though ill-gotten, this property has been singularly profitable.

"For my part, being determined to remedy the mischief, I wrote to Switzerland, and knew no peace till I was on the traces of the Protestant victim's heirs. At last I discovered that the Jeanrenauds, reduced to abject want, had left Fribourg and returned to live in France. Finally, I found a M. Jeanrenaud, lieutenant in a cavalry regiment under Napoleon, the sole heir of this unhappy family. In my eyes, monsieur, the rights of the Jeanrenauds were clear. To establish a prescriptive right is it not necessary that there should have been some possibility of proceeding against those who are in the enjoyment of it? To whom could these refugees have appealed? Their Court of Justice was on high, or rather, monsieur, it was here," and the Marquis struck his hand on his heart. "I did not choose that my children should be able to think of me as I have thought of my father and of my ancestors. I aim at leaving them an unblemished inheritance and escutcheon. I did not choose that nobility should be a lie in my person. And, after all, politically speaking, ought those emigres who are now appealing against revolutionary confiscations, to keep the property derived from antecedent confiscations by positive crimes?

"I found in M. Jeanrenaud and his mother the most perverse honesty; to hear them you would suppose that they were robbing me. In spite of all I could say, they will accept no more than the value of the lands at the time when the King bestowed them on my family. The price was settled between us at the sum of eleven hundred thousand francs, which I was to pay at my convenience and without interest. To achieve this I had to forego my income for a long time. And then, monsieur, began the destruction of some illusions I had allowed myself as to Madame d'Espard's character. When I proposed to her that we should leave Paris and go into the country, where we could live respected on half of her income, and so more rapidly complete a restitution of which I spoke to her without going into the more serious details, Madame d'Espard treated me as a madman. I then understood my wife's real character. She would have approved of my grandfather's conduct without a scruple, and have laughed at the Huguenots. Terrified by her coldness, and her little affection for her children, whom she abandoned to me without regret, I determined to leave her the command of her fortune, after paying our common debts. It was no business of hers, as she told me, to pay for my follies. As I then had not enough to live on and pay for my sons' education, I determined to educate them myself, to make them gentlemen and men of feeling. By investing my money in the funds I have been enabled to pay off my obligation sooner than I had dared to hope, for I took advantage of the opportunities afforded by the improvement in prices. If I had kept four thousand francs a year for my boys and myself, I could only have paid off twenty thousand crowns a year, and it would have taken almost eighteen years to achieve my freedom. As it is, I have lately repaid the whole of the eleven hundred thousand francs that were due. Thus I enjoy the happiness of having made this restitution without doing my children the smallest wrong.

"These, monsieur, are the reasons for the payments made to Madame Jeanrenaud and her son."

"So Madame d'Espard knew the motives of your retirement?" said the judge, controlling the emotion he felt at this narrative.

"Yes, monsieur."

Popinot gave an expressive shrug; he rose and opened the door into the next room.

"Noel, you can go," said he to his clerk.

"Monsieur," he went on, "though what you have told me is enough to enlighten me thoroughly, I should like to hear what you have to say to the other facts put forward in the petition. For instance, you are here carrying on a business such as is not habitually undertaken by a man of rank."

"We cannot discuss that matter here," said the Marquis, signing to the judge to quit the room. "Nouvion," said he to the old man, "I am going down to my rooms; the children will soon be in; dine with us."

"Then, Monsieur le Marquis," said Popinot on the stairs, "that is not your apartment?"

"No, monsieur; I took those rooms for the office of this undertaking. You see," and he pointed to an advertisement sheet, "the History is being brought out by one of the most respectable firms in Paris, and not by me."

The Marquis showed the lawyer into the ground-floor rooms, saying, "This is my apartment."

Popinot was quite touched by the poetry, not aimed at but pervading this dwelling. The weather was lovely, the windows were open, the air from the garden brought in a wholesome earthy smell, the sunshine brightened and gilded the woodwork, of a rather gloomy brown. At the sight Popinot made up his mind that a madman would hardly be capable of inventing the tender harmony of which he was at that moment conscious.

"I should like just such an apartment," thought he. "You think of leaving this part of town?" he inquired.

"I hope so," replied the Marquis. "But I shall remain till my younger son has finished his studies, and till the children's character is thoroughly formed, before introducing them to the world and to their mother's circle. Indeed, after giving them the solid information they possess, I intend to complete it by taking them to travel to the capitals of Europe, that they may see men and things, and become accustomed to speak the languages they have learned. And, monsieur," he went on, giving the judge a chair in the drawing-room, "I could not discuss the book on China with you, in the presence of an old friend of my family, the Comte de Nouvion, who, having emigrated, has returned to France without any fortune whatever, and who is my partner in this concern, less for my profit than his. Without telling him what my motives were, I explained to him that I was as poor as he, but that I had enough money to start a speculation in which he might be usefully employed. My tutor was the Abbe Grozier, whom Charles X. on my recommendation appointed Keeper of the Books at the Arsenal, which were returned to that Prince when he was still Monsieur. The Abbe Grozier was deeply learned with regard to China, its manners and customs; he made me heir to this knowledge at an age when it is difficult not to become a fanatic for the things we learn. At five-and-twenty I knew Chinese, and I confess I have never been able to check myself in an exclusive admiration for that nation, who conquered their conquerors, whose annals extend back indisputably to a period more remote than mythological or Bible times, who by their immutable institutions have preserved the integrity of their empire, whose monuments are gigantic, whose administration is perfect, among whom revolutions are impossible, who have regarded ideal beauty as a barren element in art, who have carried luxury and industry to such a pitch that we cannot outdo them in anything, while they are our equals in things where we believe ourselves superior.

"Still, monsieur, though I often make a jest of comparing China with the present condition of European states, I am not a Chinaman, I am a French gentleman. If you entertain any doubts as to the financial side of this undertaking, I can prove to you that at this moment we have two thousand five hundred subscribers to this work, which is literary, iconographical, statistical, and religious; its importance has been generally appreciated; our subscribers belong to every nation in Europe, we have but twelve hundred in France. Our book will cost about three hundred francs, and the Comte de Nouvion will derive from it from six to seven thousand francs a year, for his comfort was the real motive of the undertaking. For my part, I aimed only at the possibility of affording my children some pleasures. The hundred thousand francs I have made, quite in spite of myself, will pay for their fencing lessons, horses, dress, and theatres, pay the masters who teach them accomplishments, procure them canvases to spoil, the books they may wish to buy, in short, all the little fancies which a father finds so much pleasure in gratifying. If I had been compelled to refuse these indulgences to my poor boys, who are so good and work so hard, the sacrifice I made to the honor of my name would have been doubly painful.

"In point of fact, the twelve years I have spent in retirement from the world to educate my children have led to my being completely forgotten at Court. I have given up the career of politics; I have lost my historical fortune, and all the distinctions which I might have acquired and bequeathed to my children; but our house will have lost nothing; my boys will be men of mark. Though I have missed the senatorship, they will win it nobly by devoting themselves to the affairs of the country, and doing such service as is not soon forgotten. While purifying the past record of my family, I have insured it a glorious future; and is not that to have achieved a noble task, though in secret and without glory?--And now, monsieur, have you any other explanations to ask me?"

At this instant the tramp of horses was heard in the courtyard.

"Here they are!" said the Marquis. In a moment the two lads, fashionably but plainly dressed, came into the room, booted, spurred, and gloved, and flourishing their riding-whips. Their beaming faces brought in the freshness of the outer air; they were brilliant with health. They both grasped their father's hand, giving him a look, as friends do, a glance of unspoken affection, and then they bowed coldly to the lawyer. Popinot felt that it was quite unnecessary to question the Marquis as to his relations towards his sons.

"Have you enjoyed yourselves?" asked the Marquis.

"Yes, father; I knocked down six dolls in twelve shots at the first trial!" cried Camille.

"And where did you ride?"

"In the Bois; we saw my mother."

"Did she stop?"

"We were riding so fast just then that I daresay she did not see us," replied the young Count.

"But, then, why did you not go to speak to her?"

"I fancy I have noticed, father, that she does not care that we should speak to her in public," said Clement in an undertone. "We are a little too big."

The judge's hearing was keen enough to catch these words, which brought a cloud to the Marquis' brow. Popinot took pleasure in contemplating the picture of the father and his boys. His eyes went back with a sense of pathos to M. d'Espard's face; his features, his expression, and his manner all expressed honesty in its noblest aspect, intellectual and chivalrous honesty, nobility in all its beauty.

"You--you see, monsieur," said the Marquis, and his hesitation had returned, "you see that Justice may look in--in here at any time--yes, at any time--here. If there is anybody crazy, it can only be the children--the children--who are a little crazy about their father, and the father who is very crazy about his children--but that sort of madness rings true."

At this juncture Madame Jeanrenaud's voice was heard in the ante-room, and the good woman came bustling in, in spite of the man-servant's remonstrances.

"I take no roundabout ways, I can tell you!" she exclaimed. "Yes, Monsieur le Marquis, I want to speak to you, this very minute," she went on, with a comprehensive bow to the company. "By George, and I am too late as it is, since Monsieur the criminal Judge is before me."

"Criminal!" cried the two boys.

"Good reason why I did not find you at your own house, since you are here. Well, well! the Law is always to the fore when there is mischief brewing.--I came, Monsieur le Marquis, to tell you that my son and I are of one mind to give you everything back, since our honor is threatened. My son and I, we had rather give you back everything than cause you the smallest trouble. My word, they must be as stupid as pans without handles to call you a lunatic----"

"A lunatic! My father?" exclaimed the boys, clinging to the Marquis. "What is this?"

"Silence, madame," said Popinot.

"Children, leave us," said the Marquis.

The two boys went into the garden without a word, but very much alarmed.

"Madame," said the judge, "the moneys paid to you by Monsieur le Marquis were legally due, though given to you in virtue of a very far-reaching theory of honesty. If all the people possessed of confiscated goods, by whatever cause, even if acquired by treachery, were compelled to make restitution every hundred and fifty years, there would be few legitimate owners in France. The possessions of Jacques Coeur enriched twenty noble families; the confiscations pronounced by the English to the advantage of their adherents at the time when they held a part of France made the fortune of several princely houses.

"Our law allows M. d'Espard to dispose of his income without accounting for it, or suffering him to be accused of its misapplication. A Commission in Lunacy can only be granted when a man's actions are devoid of reason; but in this case, the remittances made to you have a reason based on the most sacred and most honorable motives. Hence you may keep it all without remorse, and leave the world to misinterpret a noble action. In Paris, the highest virtue is the object of the foulest calumny. It is, unfortunately, the present condition of society that makes the Marquis' actions sublime. For the honor of my country, I would that such deeds were regarded as a matter of course; but, as things are, I am forced by comparison to look upon M. d'Espard as a man to whom a crown should be awarded, rather than that he should be threatened with a Commission in Lunacy.

"In the course of a long professional career, I have seen and heard nothing that has touched me more deeply than that I have just seen and heard. But it is not extraordinary that virtue should wear its noblest aspect when it is practised by men of the highest class.

"Having heard me express myself in this way, I hope, Monsieur le Marquis, that you feel certain of my silence, and that you will not for a moment be uneasy as to the decision pronounced in the case--if it comes before the Court."

"There, now! Well said," cried Madame Jeanrenaud. "That is something like a judge! Look here, my dear sir, I would hug you if I were not so ugly; you speak like a book."

The Marquis held out his hand to Popinot, who gently pressed it with a look full of sympathetic comprehension at this great man in private life, and the Marquis responded with a pleasant smile. These two natures, both so large and full--one commonplace but divinely kind, the other lofty and sublime--had fallen into unison gently, without a jar, without a flash of passion, as though two pure lights had been merged into one. The father of a whole district felt himself worthy to grasp the hand of this man who was doubly noble, and the Marquis felt in the depths of his soul an instinct that told him that the judge's hand was one of those from which the treasures of inexhaustible beneficence perennially flow.

"Monsieur le Marquis," added Popinot, with a bow, "I am happy to be able to tell you that, from the first words of this inquiry, I regarded my clerk as quite unnecessary."

He went close to M. d'Espard, led him into the window-bay, and said: "It is time that you should return home, monsieur. I believe that Madame la Marquise has acted in this matter under an influence which you ought at once to counteract."

Popinot withdrew. He looked back several times as he crossed the courtyard, touched by the recollection of the scene. It was one of those which take root in the memory to blossom again in certain hours when the soul seeks consolation.

"Those rooms would just suit me," said he to himself as he reached home. "If M. d'Espard leaves them, I will take up his lease."

The next day, at about ten in the morning, Popinot, who had written out his report the previous evening, made his way to the Palais de Justice, intending to have prompt and righteous justice done. As he went to the robing-room to put on his gown and bands, the usher told him that the President of his Court begged him to attend in his private room, where he was waiting for him. Popinot forthwith obeyed.

"Good-morning, my dear Popinot," said the President, "I have been waiting for you."

"Why, Monsieur le President, is anything wrong?"

"A mere silly trifle," said the President. "The Keeper of the Seals, with whom I had the honor of dining yesterday, led me apart into a corner. He had heard that you had been to tea with Madame d'Espard, in whose case you were employed to make inquiries. He gave me to understand that it would be as well that you should not sit on this case----"

"But, Monsieur le President, I can prove that I left Madame d'Espard's house at the moment when tea was brought in. And my conscience----"

"Yes, yes; the whole Bench, the two Courts, all the profession know you. I need not repeat what I said about you to his Eminence; but, you know, 'Caesar's wife must not be suspected.' So we shall not make this foolish trifle a matter of discipline, but only of proprieties. Between ourselves, it is not on your account, but on that of the Bench."

"But, monsieur, if you only knew the kind of woman----" said the judge, trying to pull his report out of his pocket.

"I am perfectly certain that you have proceeded in this matter with the strictest independence of judgment. I myself, in the provinces, have often taken more than a cup of tea with the people I had to try; but the fact that the Keeper of the Seals should have mentioned it, and that you might be talked about, is enough to make the Court avoid any discussion of the matter. Any conflict with public opinion must always be dangerous for a constitutional body, even when the right is on its side against the public, because their weapons are not equal. Journalism may say or suppose anything, and our dignity forbids us even to reply. In fact, I have spoken of the matter to your President, and M. Camusot has been appointed in your place on your retirement, which you will signify. It is a family matter, so to speak. And I now beg you to signify your retirement from the case as a personal favor. To make up, you will get the Cross of the Legion of Honor, which has so long been due to you. I make that my business."

When he saw M. Camusot, a judge recently called to Paris from a provincial Court of the same class, as he went forward bowing to the Judge and the President, Popinot could not repress an ironical smile. This pale, fair young man, full of covert ambition, looked ready to hang and unhang, at the pleasure of any earthy king, the innocent and the guilty alike, and to follow the example of a Laubardemont rather than that of a Mole.

Popinot withdrew with a bow; he scorned to deny the lying accusation that had been brought against him.

PARIS, February 1836.

The Codes Of Hammurabi And Moses
W. W. Davies

QTY

The discovery of the Hammurabi Code is one of the greatest achievements of archaeology, and is of paramount interest, not only to the student of the Bible, but also to all those interested in ancient history...

Religion   **ISBN:** *1-59462-338-4*   **Pages:132**
MSRP $12.95

The Theory of Moral Sentiments
Adam Smith

QTY

This work from 1749. contains original theories of conscience amd moral judgment and it is the foundation for systemof morals.

Philosophy   **ISBN:** *1-59462-777-0*   **Pages:536**
MSRP $19.95

Jessica's First Prayer
Hesba Stretton

QTY

In a screened and secluded corner of one of the many railway-bridges which span the streets of London there could be seen a few years ago, from five o'clock every morning until half past eight, a tidily set-out coffee-stall, consisting of a trestle and board, upon which stood two large tin cans, with a small fire of charcoal burning under each so as to keep the coffee boiling during the early hours of the morning when the work-people were thronging into the city on their way to their daily toil...

Pages:84

Childrens   **ISBN:** *1-59462-373-2*   *MSRP $9.95*

My Life and Work
Henry Ford

QTY

Henry Ford revolutionized the world with his implementation of mass production for the Model T automobile. Gain valuable business insight into his life and work with his own auto-biography... "We have only started on our development of our country we have not as yet, with all our talk of wonderful progress, done more than scratch the surface. The progress has been wonderful enough but..."

Pages:300

Biographies/   **ISBN:** *1-59462-198-5*   *MSRP $21.95*

The Art of Cross-Examination
Francis Wellman

QTY

I presume it is the experience of every author, after his first book is published upon an important subject, to be almost overwhelmed with a wealth of ideas and illustrations which could readily have been included in his book, and which to his own mind, at least, seem to make a second edition inevitable. Such certainly was the case with me; and when the first edition had reached its sixth impression in five months, I rejoiced to learn that it seemed to my publishers that the book had met with a sufficiently favorable reception to justify a second and considerably enlarged edition. ..

Pages:412

Reference   ISBN: *1-59462-647-2*   *MSRP $19.95*

On the Duty of Civil Disobedience
Henry David Thoreau

QTY

Thoreau wrote his famous essay, On the Duty of Civil Disobedience, as a protest against an unjust but popular war and the immoral but popular institution of slave-owning. He did more than write—he declined to pay his taxes, and was hauled off to gaol in consequence. Who can say how much this refusal of his hastened the end of the war and of slavery ?

Law   ISBN: *1-59462-747-9*   **Pages:48**

MSRP $7.45

Dream Psychology Psychoanalysis for Beginners
Sigmund Freud

QTY

Sigmund Freud, born Sigismund Schlomo Freud (May 6, 1856 - September 23, 1939), was a Jewish-Austrian neurologist and psychiatrist who co-founded the psychoanalytic school of psychology. Freud is best known for his theories of the unconscious mind, especially involving the mechanism of repression; his redefinition of sexual desire as mobile and directed towards a wide variety of objects; and his therapeutic techniques, especially his understanding of transference in the therapeutic relationship and the presumed value of dreams as sources of insight into unconscious desires.

Pages:196

Psychology   ISBN: *1-59462-905-6*   *MSRP $15.45*

The Miracle of Right Thought
Orison Swett Marden

QTY

Believe with all of your heart that you will do what you were made to do. When the mind has once formed the habit of holding cheerful, happy, prosperous pictures, it will not be easy to form the opposite habit. It does not matter how improbable or how far away this realization may see, or how dark the prospects may be, if we visualize them as best we can, as vividly as possible, hold tenaciously to them and vigorously struggle to attain them, they will gradually become actualized, realized in the life. But a desire, a longing without endeavor, a yearning abandoned or held indifferently will vanish without realization.

Pages:360

Self Help   ISBN: *1-59462-644-8*   *MSRP $25.45*

QTY

☐ **The Rosicrucian Cosmo-Conception Mystic Christianity** *by Max Heindel*   ISBN: *1-59462-188-8*   **$38.95**
The Rosicrucian Cosmo-conception is not dogmatic, neither does it appeal to any other authority than the reason of the student. It is; not controversial, but is: sent forth in the, hope that it may help to clear...   *New Age/Religion Pages 646*

☐ **Abandonment To Divine Providence** *by Jean-Pierre de Caussade*   ISBN: *1-59462-228-0*   **$25.95**
"The Rev. Jean Pierre de Caussade was one of the most remarkable spiritual writers of the Society of Jesus in France in the 18th Century. His death took place at Toulouse in 1751. His works have gone through many editions and have been republished...   *Inspirational/Religion Pages 400*

☐ **Mental Chemistry** *by Charles Haanel*   ISBN: *1-59462-192-6*   **$23.95**
Mental Chemistry allows the change of material conditions by combining and appropriately utilizing the power of the mind. Much like applied chemistry creates something new and unique out of careful combinations of chemicals the mastery of mental chemistry...   *New Age Pages 354*

☐ **The Letters of Robert Browning and Elizabeth Barret Barrett 1845-1846 vol II**   ISBN: *1-59462-193-4*   **$35.95**
by Robert Browning and Elizabeth Barrett   *Biographies Pages 596*

☐ **Gleanings In Genesis (volume I)** *by Arthur W. Pink*   ISBN: *1-59462-130-6*   **$27.45**
Appropriately has Genesis been termed "the seed plot of the Bible" for in it we have, in germ form, almost all of the great doctrines which are afterwards fully developed in the books of Scripture which follow.   *Religion/Inspirational Pages 420*

☐ **The Master Key** *by L. W. de Laurence*   ISBN: *1-59462-001-6*   **$30.95**
In no branch of human knowledge has there been a more lively increase of the spirit of research during the past few years than in the study of Psychology, Concentration and Mental Discipline. The requests for authentic lessons in Thought Control, Mental Discipline and...   *New Age/Business Pages 422*

☐ **The Lesser Key Of Solomon Goetia** *by L. W. de Laurence*   ISBN: *1-59462-092-X*   **$9.95**
This translation of the first book of the "Lernegton" which is now for the first time made accessible to students of Talismanic Magic was done, after careful collation and edition, from numerous Ancient Manuscripts in Hebrew, Latin, and French...   *New Age/Occult Pages 92*

☐ **Rubaiyat Of Omar Khayyam** *by Edward Fitzgerald*   ISBN: *1-59462-332-5*   **$13.95**
Edward Fitzgerald, whom the world has already learned, in spite of his own efforts to remain within the shadow of anonymity, to look upon as one of the rarest poets of the century, was born at Bredfield, in Suffolk, on the 31st of March, 1809. He was the third son of John Purcell...   *Music Pages 172*

☐ **Ancient Law** *by Henry Maine*   ISBN: *1-59462-128-4*   **$29.95**
The chief object of the following pages is to indicate some of the earliest ideas of mankind, as they are reflected in Ancient Law, and to point out the relation of those ideas to modern thought.   *Religion/History Pages 452*

☐ **Far-Away Stories** *by William J. Locke*   ISBN: *1-59462-129-2*   **$19.45**
"Good wine needs no bush, but a collection of mixed vintages does. And this book is just such a collection. Some of the stories I do not want to remain buried for ever in the museum files of dead magazine-numbers an author's not unpardonable vanity..."   *Fiction Pages 272*

☐ **Life of David Crockett** *by David Crockett*   ISBN: *1-59462-250-7*   **$27.45**
"Colonel David Crockett was one of the most remarkable men of the times in which he lived. Born in humble life, but gifted with a strong will, an indomitable courage, and unremitting perseverance...   *Biographies/New Age Pages 424*

☐ **Lip-Reading** *by Edward Nitchie*   ISBN: *1-59462-206-X*   **$25.95**
Edward B. Nitchie, founder of the New York School for the Hard of Hearing, now the Nitchie School of Lip-Reading, Inc, wrote "LIP-READING Principles and Practice". The development and perfecting of this meritorious work on lip-reading was an undertaking...   *How-to Pages 400*

☐ **A Handbook of Suggestive Therapeutics, Applied Hypnotism, Psychic Science**   ISBN: *1-59462-214-0*   **$24.95**
by Henry Munro   *Health/New Age/Health/Self-help Pages 376*

☐ **A Doll's House: and Two Other Plays** *by Henrik Ibsen*   ISBN: *1-59462-112-8*   **$19.95**
Henrik Ibsen created this classic when in revolutionary 1848 Rome. Introducing some striking concepts in playwriting for the realist genre, this play has been studied the world over.   *Fiction/Classics/Plays 308*

☐ **The Light of Asia** *by sir Edwin Arnold*   ISBN: *1-59462-204-3*   **$13.95**
In this poetic masterpiece, Edwin Arnold describes the life and teachings of Buddha. The man who was to become known as Buddha to the world was born as Prince Gautama of India but he rejected the worldly riches and abandoned the reigns of power when...   *Religion/History/Biographies Pages 170*

☐ **The Complete Works of Guy de Maupassant** *by Guy de Maupassant*   ISBN: *1-59462-157-8*   **$16.95**
"For days and days, nights and nights, I had dreamed of that first kiss which was to consecrate our engagement, and I knew not on what spot I should put my lips..."   *Fiction/Classics Pages 240*

☐ **The Art of Cross-Examination** *by Francis L. Wellman*   ISBN: *1-59462-309-0*   **$26.95**
Written by a renowned trial lawyer, Wellman imparts his experience and uses case studies to explain how to use psychology to extract desired information through questioning.   *How-to/Science/Reference Pages 408*

☐ **Answered or Unanswered?** *by Louisa Vaughan*   ISBN: *1-59462-248-5*   **$10.95**
Miracles of Faith in China   *Religion Pages 112*

☐ **The Edinburgh Lectures on Mental Science (1909)** *by Thomas*   ISBN: *1-59462-008-3*   **$11.95**
This book contains the substance of a course of lectures recently given by the writer in the Queen Street Hail, Edinburgh. Its purpose is to indicate the Natural Principles governing the relation between Mental Action and Material Conditions...   *New Age/Psychology Pages 148*

☐ **Ayesha** *by H. Rider Haggard*   ISBN: *1-59462-301-5*   **$24.95**
Verily and indeed it is the unexpected that happens! Probably if there was one person upon the earth from whom the Editor of this, and of a certain previous history, did not expect to hear again...   *Classics Pages 380*

☐ **Ayala's Angel** *by Anthony Trollope*   ISBN: *1-59462-352-X*   **$29.95**
The two girls were both pretty, but Lucy who was twenty-one who supposed to be simple and comparatively unattractive, whereas Ayala was credited, as her Bombwhat romantic name might show, with poetic charm and a taste for romance. Ayala when her father died was nineteen...   *Fiction Pages 484*

☐ **The American Commonwealth** *by James Bryce*   ISBN: *1-59462-286-8*   **$34.45**
An interpretation of American democratic political theory. It examines political mechanics and society from the perspective of Scotsman James Bryce   *Politics Pages 572*

☐ **Stories of the Pilgrims** *by Margaret P. Pumphrey*   ISBN: *1-59462-116-0*   **$17.95**
This book explores pilgrims religious oppression in England as well as their escape to Holland and eventual crossing to America on the Mayflower, and their early days in New England...   *History Pages 268*

QTY

The Fasting Cure *by Sinclair Upton*   ISBN: *1-59462-222-1* **$13.95**
*In the Cosmopolitan Magazine for May, 1910, and in the Contemporary Review (London) for April, 1910, I published an article dealing with my experi-
ences in fasting. I have written a great many magazine articles, but never one which attracted so much attention... New Age/Self Help/Health Pages 101*

Hebrew Astrology *by Sepharial*   ISBN: *1-59462-308-2* **$13.45**
*In these days of advanced thinking it is a matter of common observation that we have left many of the old landmarks behind and that we are now pressing
forward to greater heights and to a wider horizon than that which represented the mind-content of our progenitors...   Astrology Pages 144*

Thought Vibration or The Law of Attraction in the Thought World   ISBN: *1-59462-127-6* **$12.95**
by William Walker Atkinson   *Psychology/Religion Pages 144*

Optimism *by Helen Keller*   ISBN: *1-59462-108-X* **$15.95**
*Helen Keller was blind, deaf, and mute since 19 months old, yet famously learned how to overcome these handicaps, communicate with the world, and
spread her lectures promoting optimism. An inspiring read for everyone...   Biographies/Inspirational Pages 84*

Sara Crewe *by Frances Burnett*   ISBN: *1-59462-360-0*   **$9.45**
*In the first place, Miss Minchin lived in London. Her home was a large, dull, tall one, in a large, dull square, where all the houses were alike, and all the
sparrows were alike, and where all the door-knockers made the same heavy sound...   Childrens/Classic Pages 88*

The Autobiography of Benjamin Franklin *by Benjamin Franklin*   ISBN: *1-59462-135-7* **$24.95**
*The Autobiography of Benjamin Franklin has probably been more extensively read than any other American historical work, and no other book of its kind
has had such ups and downs of fortune. Franklin lived for many years in England, where he was agent...   Biographies/History Pages 332*

Name	
Email	
Telephone	
Address	
City, State ZIP	

☐ **Credit Card**   ☐ **Check / Money Order**

Credit Card Number	
Expiration Date	
Signature	

Please Mail to: *Book Jungle*
PO Box 2226
Champaign, IL 61825
or Fax to: *630-214-0564*

ORDERING INFORMATION

web*: www.bookjungle.com*
email*: sales@bookjungle.com*
fax*: 630-214-0564*
mail*: Book Jungle PO Box 2226 Champaign, IL 61825*
or PayPal *to sales@bookjungle.com*

Please contact us for bulk discounts

DIRECT-ORDER TERMS

**20% Discount if You Order
Two or More Books**
Free Domestic Shipping!
Accepted: Master Card, Visa,
Discover, American Express